*T*WELVE
*C*HRISTMAS *G*IFTS
... FROM CUSHING, MAINE

BY
JUDITH M. KNOWLTON

QUOTIDIAN PUBLISHERS
377 RIVER ROAD
CUSHING, MAINE
04563

2008

Passing Sophie: 1996
The Lady & the Lighthouse: 1997
The Cat Who Caught Christmas: 1998
The Serene Season: 1999
Just Where Does Cushing Begin? 2000
Creatures with Long Green Tails: 2001
The Gift in Gamma's Garden: 2002
Holiday Lights: 2003
Wonder!: 2004
Lunch with Luthera: 2005
A Flock of Hope: 2006
Flying High: 2007
The Fragrance of Christmas: 2008

*C*ONTENTS

Season's Greetings

Now is the time of the Winter Solstice. About December 21, the sunrise reaches it's southern-most point on the horizon, and seems actually to *stand still* (the meaning of solstice), marking the shortest day of the year.

Each morning, my habit is to note where the first red gleam eases between the trees at the far end of my back yard. On winter solstice, the sun pauses for a couple of days exactly between the twin trunks of a specific tree.

Probably every culture celebrates the sun's hesitation, as it appears to reverse and then make its way toward spring. No wonder we celebrate! Long before Jesus was born, we humans were hailing this marker of the rebirth of the earth.

People often celebrate with gifts. This book consists of 12 essays that I wrote between 1996 and 2007, then mailed or hand-delivered to my friends and neighbors -- a personally designed Christmas card, so to speak. The last one is new – for Christmas Eve.

Not all of these essays have holiday themes, but each defines gift giving in some fashion. This year, I've added the "Fragrance of Christmas," to complete the collection. It perfectly describes my understanding that it is more blessed to give than to receive. And, because it is a true story about three of my grandchildren, it has special meaning for me.

Regardless of your faith, may I wish you the joys of the Season, and simple pleasures with loved ones, whether they be humans or adored creatures, Each is a unique gift from our Creator to us. I am grateful that I can keep all such gifts whole in my memory, even years after they have left my view.

And may your hope be restored, knowing that the earth is preparing for it's annual renewal.

Judy Knowlton
Cushing, Maine - 2008

Why a Snow-Decked Wreath?

Holidays are times for ritual and tradition.

The Christmas I moved to Maine, I bought a wreath at our local church Fair. It was full and fragrant, the evergreens remarkably soft and fresh, scattered with deep red winterberries. Jeannette Chapman told me it was one of her creations. She's been making these symbols of renewal and infinity for perhaps 40 years! Instantly it became my tradition to be at the Fair the moment the doors open, to rush to buy one – because they vanish about as quickly as her famous doughnut holes!

The photograph on the cover is wreath number twelve. I wanted to acknowledge the pleasure her gifts give me. And they *are* gifts. She traipses the local fields in late fall, gathering the greens. The finished wreaths are her gift to her church; the price I pay is really another gift. The crisp, clean odor of fresh evergreens fills my car with the reminder of Christmases past, and that is my gift to my own self. Then I hang it at my door, to welcome all the friends who enter my home over the holidays.

You may wonder why this wreath is decked with icicles and snow. Does it make you shiver just to look at it? It's a reminder of the winter of 2007 and 2008 – weather like the storms of my youth in New Jersey! Every few days another snow, another set of gray days, another driveway plowing.

Predicting the Winter's Snowstorms

Here in Cushing, we have a traditional way to predict the winter's snows. Some say that the Abenaki Indians used a similar system. A "snow" is recorded when it is deep enough to show a cat's track. Sadly, I can't use my own two cats as measuring devices, because they refuse to stick their noses beyond the door jam if the air even *smells* of snow!!

Predictions are based on 3 measures:
First: the day of the first snowfall.

(This year it was December 3rd.)	**3**
Add the age of the moon (from "new"):	**24**
Add the day of the week (Sunday is the first)	**1 or 2**

Total them up. Fales Store recorded this prediction during the '07-'08 winter: **28 or 29**

There's seems to be some controversy over when a week begins. John Fales says Monday, but the Calendar week begins on Sunday. It's your choice.

And just how accurate is this time-honored system?

This year we counted **39** cat-trackable snowfalls.

Most were so deep my cats refused to set foot!

Coloring the Covers

The artwork for each of these stories was printed in line drawings of black-and-white. Each was hand-tinted by me, in one or two colors. Why not think of this as your own coloring book? Here's what I did:

Passing Sophie: Here, a floating cherub was intended, but she was beyond my artistic abilities!

The Lady & the Lighthouse: A red scarf, and perhaps a red ribbon on a green wreath.

The Cat Who Caught Christmas: Just a red flower.

The Serene Season: A stark black and white winter.

Just Where Does Cushing Begin? A flame with an orange center and yellow outer edge.

Creatures with Long Green Tails: Red holly berries and a leaf lightly edged in green.

The Gift in Gamma's Garden: Green leaves and a Pink flower, leaving the "drop" white.

Holiday Lights: a yellow light and halo.

Wonder!   I left it clean -- in pristine black and white.

Lunch with Luthera: Just a red ribbon around the silverware.

A Flock of Hope: Two yellow chicks – nothing more.

Flying High: The kite, a bright color; the tail can be multi-colored bows.

The Fragrance of Christmas: Why even attempt to draw a cake? After all, the joy is in the flavor, texture and fragrance!

* * *

$\mathcal{P}$ASSING $\mathcal{S}$OPHIE

OR
AN ANGEL'S CHRISTMAS BLESSING

My feet ached. The chapel in the woods exuded chill air from the stone wall at our backs, and wisps of frozen breath rose toward the raftered roof. Music sheets held with mitten-hands, smiling into each others' eyes, we brave carolers welcomed the Christ Child's birth again this year. "I love coming here to Columcille," I was thinking. "Visiting this chapel so close to my home in the Pocono Mountains is a tradition I've invented for myself now that I live alone."

And then we turned the page and struck the first slow, glorious, measured tones of the most famous carol of all, "Silent night, holy night..."

My throat constricted. I couldn't make a sound. The faces in front of me blurred. An icicle slammed into the back of my neck and there I was, kneeling beside my only brother – my children's "Uncle John." We were sharing a hymnal, shoulder to shoulder at our crowded midnight service, our voices weaving alto as the clear soprano voices of the boys' choir soared around us in our childhood church of stone and stained glass, formal and Episcopal. I knew it was the last Christmas before my brother died. In another instant I was a tiny child, standing on the pew seat between my mother and my grandmother, in a simple Congregational Church in New England, my Gamma's arm tight around my waist as the melody surrounded us: "...sleep in heavenly peace." I leaned against her and looked into her face, mesmerized by the stars of candlelight glinting from her octagonal eyeglasses

11

beneath the shadow of a grand black felt hat – an old-fashioned relic even to my five-year-old mind in 1940.

But I'm sixty now and it's the winter of ninety-five. Without warning, I was back in the chapel, carol music humming in my ears. Had I been silently mouthing the words? I have no idea. Every year it's harder to face the holiday season because of those poignant flashbacks. Why do the memories come so easily now, when they used to hide in the recesses of my mind? A lump settles in my throat around Thanksgiving time and stays until the Big Apple ball falls in Times Square on New Year's Eve.

Don't for a moment think I'm consumed with sadness. Hardly that. It's just this holiday season thing – memories of a lengthening life that took a new course a few years ago at my daughter Caroline's house. One warm spring day I became "Gamma" myself. Such an ordinary experience, but it thrilled me. A small hand tugged at mine with urgency. "Gamma, Gamma, come. I show you." Two-year-old Andrew dragged me up the stairs to his room to admire some treasure, and we frolicked. (I hadn't forgotten how to frolic!) I've become a horse, a whale, a sofa. We've commandeered a fleet of walnut shell ships with paper sails (toothpicks stuck in candle wax) and constructed marble slides from building blocks. Sometimes waves of unconditional love radiate from my heart and for long moments I forget how to judge or control or bark orders. If only I'd known these things when my own children and I struggled to grow up, three long decades ago! Back then, I simply didn't know what was important and what didn't matter. Now my hair is long and gray, and I twist it up contentedly because I'm a "Gamma" – and the role fits me a little better every day.

* * *

Andrew has a baby sister, born during one of the blizzards of '94 that swept across the land every week like clockwork that year, eighteen in all. On February ninth Caroline and the family barely made it to Manhattan. Then they were thrown out of the hospital 24 hours later (money having become more important than babies!) and the blizzard prevented them from reaching Connecticut. Thankfully they found a hotel room in the crowded city, (yes, a room at the inn!), and the newborn was warmly loved by the hotel staff.

For two full days this little child had no name. How strange that nothing her parents chose seemed to fit. At last my daughter phoned me. "Her name is Sophie, and you'll know why when you see her." Two years later, I do indeed understand, because Sophie means "wisdom." Even total strangers will say to Caroline: "Ah, how beautiful she is – one of this new breed of children who will lead us into peace." You recognize these children instantly because their souls are aglow with hope and serenity and joy. My daughter accepts such comments because she hears them time and again, but they still make the hairs on the back of my neck prickle. Anyway, it's more than just the pride of a grandmother saying that Sophie is unique.

By Christmas morning, I'd pushed my melancholy aside and felt like a modern-day Santa, loaded down with a plastic garbage bag full of gifts and swept up (at last!) into the spirit of the season – a perfect day, with just enough snow on the ground for atmosphere. When I arrived, my daughter's home in Connecticut was already a mass of wrappings and toys and two little children swimming in a sea of laughter. Caroline and her husband Henry have created a home of welcome and love, and a new Christmas tradition just as wonderful. Every year since Andrew was born, the same people have gathered – Henry's brother Bryan and his

13

wife Christine, David from Boston and Lisa from New York and Caroline's closest friend Amy. We've dubbed it our Jewish Christmas, and it's opened up a universe for me, because these close friends bring no "Ghosts of Christmas Past" as I do. They have no vision of "how Christmas is supposed to look." They come just for the love of Henry and Caroline and Andrew and Sophie, and so they bring with them and are greeted by and share together the true meaning of Christmas. We gather this love around us like a warm blanket.

Of course new acts have joyfully become old traditions. Each year we unwrap one gift at a time and savor each one. Eat-breakfast-clean-up-unwrap-gifts-oh-and-ah-consume-lunch-do-all-the-kitchen-chores-take-a-coffee-break-clean-up-children-nap-grown-ups-walk-more-unwrapping.

Then Caroline and David take over the kitchen and we wait, stuffed and drowsy, for the *real* banquet to begin. (I'm salivating even now as I write!)

This Christmas of ninety-five, eight adults and two young children gathered in the dining room and held hands for a moment of thanks around a the table loaded with savory dishes. Andrew had his own full-size chair, and Sophie's little chair seat lifted her to table height. Outside, the lights of neighbors' living rooms shone dimly in the dusk, while inside, the faces around the table were gently lit by candlelight.

Sophie is a true charmer – a witty young lady with wise eyes and bouncing blonde curls who knows her own mind. But don't ask her to wear clothes in the house, because she simply won't do it. Despite some gorgeous new Christmas outfits, she came to the table in her all-together and disposable diapers. Earlier, when her father suggested she put on a new outfit, she shook her head emphatically "no!" Then he asked slyly, "May I take your picture?

Instant personality change! She eagerly clambered

14

into her new clothes and posed with gleeful zest, only to zip out of them again the moment he put the camera down. Twenty-two months worth of iron-willed determination!

And then it happened. Someone said, "Please pass the butter," and someone else asked for beans. And then I think it was Henry who said "Pass Sophie." Later on, Caroline said to me, "That was really bizarre, wasn't it? I wonder what someone walking by outside would think!"

"Maybe it *was* odd," "I answered her, still in a daze, "but let me tell you what I saw."

Caroline had lifted this almost-naked little child into the air and handed her to Christine, who swung her gently around and passed her over to me. Each of us held her reverently and upright, high above our heads so her feet would miss dishes and candles. Sophie sailed slowly above the table, her arms outstretched, a living replica of every plaster-creche Christ-child, plump and bare except for her shining disposable loincloth. A demure Mona Lisa smile played across her face as the walls of the dining room receded into shadows behind her, allowing a Rembrandt gleam of candlelight to intensify her smooth skin and pale curls and huge wise eyes.

She returned at last to the bosom of her mother but, not finished with us yet, stretched her little arms out insistently to Christine again. This time around, a living baroque cherub smiled serenely at me from her elevated place above the table, stretched out her arms again and blessed us all. The room grew steadily brighter until the radiance expanded far into the snowy night. Then Caroline slid Sophie onto her little high-seat, and, completely unruffled, the little girl reached for some food on her plate.

Thoroughly bewildered, I leaned across in front of Christine to stare at this child who had circled above us all with such poise and trust. Suddenly Sophie tipped her head and glanced out of the corner of her eye with a roguish grin. She scrunched up her little shoulders as if hugging herself

15

with glee. Then she looked me straight in the eye and laughed aloud, and ducked her head to go on eating as if to say, "We have a secret, don't we, Gamma?"

* * *

The following month a blizzard imprisoned me for four days and then let loose raging torrents down the Delaware. The saplings along the river's edge were stripped of their bark, leaving pale yellow skeletons bent flat by the floods. These were difficult times for the land and its creatures, but the message of Christmas this year had settled deep into my heart, calming my fears and softening my sadness. I was renewed by the clear knowledge that, despite our hardships, we are all loved. Tiny Tim's blessing was never more heartfelt or powerful.

This is the stuff of family legends.

Every year when we've gathered in the dining room and held hands, someone is bound to ask, "Remember the year we passed Sophie around the Christmas table?" I expect us all to murmur happily. Perhaps Andrew will nod wisely because, after all, he was there. Sophie will come to believe she remembers it too, even if she doesn't really.

I only know that my life has been profoundly touched by the blessing of that small angel, and when my faith waivers even slightly, the memory of Sophie's absolutely trusting smile comes unbidden to my mind and lifts me up again. It assures me that, in the shared love of family and friends, our spirits are safe.

XXX

The LADY & the
LIGHTHOUSE
A CHRISTMAS FABLE FOR ADULTS

THE *Lady*
AND THE *Lighthouse*

Not a dite o' Christmas spirit in me," the white-haired woman muttered to herself as she rinsed her mug and set it in the rack to dry. "Not like the cheerful me at all. Just another old biddy talking to herself. Pretty soon my bones will be predicting the weather." She was thankful that hadn't happened yet; her tall, thin body was sure evidence of good health and Maine heritage. "Seventy two," her monologue continued. "Truly a tough old bird." Usually this idea pleased her, but today she merely shook her head. How fast her life was racing by! Children scattered to the four points of the compass and dear Albert J. gone all these many years. What in heaven's name is the point of it all? The old woman sighed furtively so as not to admit the depth of her despondency even to herself, but the truth was that Etta Leighton felt very much alone.

She peered out the sitting room window toward the tidal cove, unpleasantly surprised to see only soft, pearl gray nothingness. The rounded granite rocks and stark pines on the far side of the water, even her favorite twisted apple tree close to the house – all had been blotted out by the fog. "Pea soup! And on Christmas Eve!" Etta declared sharply. It was the last pricking straw of a hollow holiday.

"I simply *must* get out of this house!" she grumbled, hauling on her black coat and boots, thinking how well the lack

21

of color suited her mood. In a burst of bravado, she wrapped a Christmas-red scarf about her neck and flipped the ends over each shoulder. "It's hard to put on airs when you only have a scarf," she said aloud, smiling wanly as she imagined how Albert J. would've enjoyed that odd play on words.

Outside, the air was so full of moisture that she impulsively reached up and tested it between her thumb and forefinger. The spring-like weather had turned her icy drive to slush, and she steadied herself with one hand on the hood of her purple four-wheeler. Her Puritan-bred mother would've been horrified by the brash color of the vehicle, "Although," as Etta noted with some regret, "it isn't powerfully purple at all – more like the sky at dusk after a glorious sunset."

The snow on the windshield slid in neatly folded pleats onto the wipers. Scooping the mush away, she patted the fender fondly. "When the world was young ... and so was I," as she liked to say, "my car was an impatient stallion eager to carry me to freedom and adventure." And it still *was*! Selling a car was traumatic. She would talk remorsefully to it on the way to the dealer's, apologize for rejecting it, repeating profuse good-byes and thanks for its faithful service. Silly? Perhaps, but the ritual had meaning for her – and yet she knew better than to admit this eccentricity out loud to anyone!

The elderly woman slid easily behind the wheel, and instantly inhaled the piquant sweet odor of ever-greens that filled the vehicle. "Oh my ... the wreath!" Etta was dismayed. She'd bought it at the church Christmas sale a couple of weeks ago but never hung it. Every year she stood in line early and eagerly for the biggest wreath and yet ... this year she'd simply forgotten it on the floor of her car.   The purple steed swung onto slick asphalt and soon the driver found herself – eyes squinting into the fog and shoulders hunched intently over the wheel – drawn down a doubtful road. "Where am I and what the dickens is going on?"

Truthfully, she was not that much puzzled by this urgent need to brave the fog. Long ago she'd learned to act on these curious impulses – Providential Pushes she liked to call them – because good things swept into her life as a result. But on this Christmas Eve, melancholy dampened her usual attitude of childlike expectation.

Suddenly a tiny triangular plot of land with a flag pole and war memorial emerged from the gray world and then, less distinctly, a doll-size shop front with an oversize window proclaiming *Owl's Head General Store.* "Oh, ho!" Etta exclaimed. "This horse still knows the way!" She turned at the old post office and again onto Lighthouse Road, recalling countless times when she, the Perennial Maine Guide, drove here in the summer sun with a car full of chattering house guests. Her day trip was certain to include Mt. Battie, an antique store or two, Camden and Rockland Harbors, time out for a lobster roll, a stroll through the Farnsworth Museum – and the lighthouse. Etta sniffed rather than laughing outright. In all her years, she swore, she'd never tired of The Tour.

Swinging a sharp left at the weathered wooden sign:

SLOW 15 mph,

the car crept past the cemetery on the jostling washboard of a dirt road. She hauled on the brake, swung open the door, and was instantly greeted by the tenor voice of the foghorn:

HOOOOO. HOOOOO.

By now Etta was talking earnestly to herself. "I must be here for a reason. What can it be?" Again the scent of evergreens caught in her nostrils. "The wreath? The lighthouse needs a *Christmas ornament*? That's absurd!" But she reached for it with nary a thought and slid the fragrant ring over her arm, failing to notice that the merest odor of evergreen had dissolved some of her depression.

The white-haired woman inched along the slippery road by clinging to the board fence, pausing to heed the gentle lap-

lapping of waves on the beach rocks at the base of the granite cliff far below. "I wonder if the Vinalhaven ferry is running in this weather. Wouldn't the waves be stronger if a ship were passing? Imagine missing Christmas with your family just because there was no ferry to carry you home!" Etta plodded on until she caught the barest glimmer of light above the pines. Nowadays the beacon always shines, even in daytime. It was doubtful that the dim spark could be seen on Mussel Ridge today. Could it even pierce a fog at night?

HOOOOO. HOOOOO.

"Silly," Etta chided herself, "Its *foghorns* that are designed to handle this fog!" The insistent, steady voice of Owl's Head Light was louder now. "Sounds just like its name," the old lady decided. Then, faintly over the water came the single note of Rockland's breakwater, as the two lighthouses reassured each other across the green-black glassy harbor, concealed completely now by the thickening mist. These lights were navigational points, in the words of an old hymn, "for those in peril on the sea." They warned ships of the dangers of jagged rocks and shallows, or signaled them to safe harbor.
"So many wrecks over the years," Etta thought idly. "Rough rocks and torturous tides. Terrifying – and yet so many lives saved because of the lights too." As a little girl, she'd fallen asleep many a night to the lowing of off-shore foghorns. Soothing they were, and she thought of them as sounds of security – a true Maine child's lullaby.

HOOOO! HOOOO!

This louder tenor voice startled the old woman. She had reached the gate with its terse message:

Closed at Sunset; U.S. Coast Guard

But it was still daylight and the gate was wide open to her. She took aim at the barely glimmering beacon in the distance, clutched her red-ribboned wreath and slid down the slope and past the light-keeper's house. The effort wore her down. She rested awhile against the stair rail, taking deep breaths, then hauled herself up eight wooden steps to read the historical marker. The beacon was first lit September 10, 1825. "My birthday plus exactly a hundred years!" Even now, Etta believed that she and the lighthouse were somehow related by their common birthdays. Shifting the wreath up to her shoulder, she started along the sloping ramp. The old woman's knees were weak, but she was no longer feeling in the least cranky. Far above her the lighthouse stood proudly in the mist, dressed in white brick robes with gleaming face and black cap – like a choirboy preparing to sing his Christmas solo. "Well, I'm crazy as a coot!" Etta exclaimed, shaking her head at this preposterous image, and yet knowing it was not so foolish to bring this lighted sentinel a gift.

Every ten seconds the lighthouse voice boomed out:

HOOOO! HOOOO!

At the top of the long ramp, her efforts were challenged by a steep flight of wooden stairs, and a warning:

~ Caution ~
Sound signal may sound
automatically without warning.
Sound pressure levels beyond
this point may be hazardous
to your health.

"What am I to do? Aha! I'll count about eight seconds ...stop...clamp both hands over ears ... wait ... and then take a few more steps!" And so she began the long, slow climb to the light. "...seven eight ..." pause ... hands on ears. (Muffled: Hoooo! Hoooo!) then on again and up, shifting the wreath, heaving forward hand-over-hand, thinking how crazy this must look to any stranger below. "Forty nine ... fifty ... *fifty one*!" Etta stood dizzily on the last step, heart pounding, out of breath but victorious. "I thought I could!" she whispered in triumph and clapped her hands sharply over her ears in the nick of time.

WHO! WHO!

The question didn't surprise her. "It's only me, Al," the old lady called back – quite as if she were conversing with her husband Albert J., and besides, people who lived here often said it quickly – "Al's Head." Perhaps giving this lighthouse the name of Al wasn't too farfetched after all. "I was feeling so down," she went on. "No holiday spirit. And I thought, well ... you might like a Christmas present." (Hands swiftly over her ears.)

WHO! YOU?

"Ehyuh, it's a gift from me to you, Al. But I don't see a hook on the door. Haven't you ever had a wreath before? There you stand, in every kind of weather, doing your duty. A lonely and thankless job – especially with automation, eh? No one tends your flame any more, or polishes your reflector every night and cleans off the smoke." The old lady propped the circle of greens against the door, spreading the red ribbon neatly on the step. "There now. You're dressed full." She wondered vaguely if she were honoring her husband or the lighthouse. "Merry Christmas, Al."

YOU! TOO!

Etta's holiday depression vanished. The humor of this exchange sparked a laugh that rose from deep inside her, exploded and soared joyfully above the harbor. Yes, the old Etta was back. Only then did she realize that the foghorn was vibrating her whole insides – her heart and lungs, stomach and brain. It frightened her. "I'm going to talk to you from the cellar, Al," she explained, pointing down the long flight of stairs. "I'm too close to your booming voice."

Going down was far easier than climbing, especially without the wreath, but her legs shook from the strain. Every few seconds the old woman repeated the familiar behavior: step, step, step, pause, cover ears, step, step – as the lighthouse called forth its rhythmic warning. At the bottom she heaved a sigh and collapsed onto the wet tread, caring nothing for the state of her coat.

Elbows propped on her knees, she cupped her palms protectively over her ears. "The fact is, Al..." she continued the conversation in this position, "You're much more than a warning beacon. You're all the things I should be striving for – especially at Christmas. Why, I believe you *are* the Spirit of Christmas!"

WOOO! WOOO!

"Are you flabbergasted? But you care for strangers, don't you? And never expect thanks? Reach out to them regardless of who they are? Show your willingness in all kinds

27

of weather? And never *ever* give up? That's called unconditional love, Al. Why, it's the Golden Rule and the true meaning of Christmas all wrapped up in one!" A cool breeze touched her face and Etta shivered, not from the shifting weather but from delight. Never before this moment had she truly understood why people are drawn to lighthouses.

TOO! TOO!

"I know that I'm supposed to reach out, too. But it's so hard, Al. I'm tired and alone. Everyone I love is distant or gone. No one needs an old lady on Christmas Eve!" Etta's dark emotions tore at her once again, but this time they were clearly wrapped in self-pity. High time to push them away and take action. But even attending her beloved candlelight service at church didn't seem important. What could she do that would truly matter? Just then the simple idea: "help someone," drifted through the old woman's mind. She sat bolt upright and dropped her hands.

YOU! YOU!

"Don't push me, Al," Etta answered a bit tersely. "I know exactly what I need to do. The Morrills would love to go to the candlelight service, but their little girl is sick. I'll baby-sit for them this evening." As if on cue, a gust of cold air swirled around the light-house headland, thinning the fog and intensifying the light of the winter sun. She spun around slowly, blinking in the brightness. "Hello, God!" She cried. "Are You giving me a sign? How trite. . .and yet how glorious," she added, laughing wildly and stretching her arms up to the sky. "Yes! I'm listening to You!"

WHO? DO!

"Well, I never! Corrected by a lighthouse! Ehyuh, you set me to rights, Al. Don't worry; I'll never forget that."

The old woman paused on her way back to the parking lot, to watch the fog fade and the rocks and pines along the shore spring into sharp focus. A chill wind ruffled patches on the ocean's surface, and in the distance the Vinalhaven ferry plied its way through the dark green water off Owl's Head. She was energized by her plan to visit the Morrills and failed to notice that the lighthouse
had fallen suddenly silent in the sun.

* * *

By the time Etta arrived at the Morrill's old cape, she was filled with the spirit of giving. Andrew, their oldest boy, opened the door. "It's Miss Etta," he called out, reaching up to give her a hug. Father Jonathan welcomed the elderly woman into their home, bending down for a respectful peck on the cheek. "We didn't expect to see you before Christmas, Etta. Come warm up by the stove."

"Isn't your tree beautiful!" Etta exclaimed, clapping her hands and admiring the child-made popcorn chains and paper ornaments. Little Sophie scooted about among the family, her gold curls bouncing. "I made that one, Mizzetta, See? See?" She pointed proudly to a crayoned paper ball tied on the lowest branch with red ribbon.

Mother Jenny, looking very pregnant and over- tired, said, "Sophie, fetch Miss Etta that tiny little box with the gold ribbon."

The child was too excited to sit still. When Etta had seated herself, Sophie climbed instantly into her lap. "Open it now, Mizzetta. Open, open! Four hands working in a flurry of cross-purposes, they finally untied the ribbon and lifted the lid.

29

"Oh, how lovely!" Etta whispered. On the tissue paper lay a red-enamel poinsettia pin with a bright green leaf. Jenny smiled. "I thought of you and your red scarf," she explained.

Before the visitor could say thank you, the little girl demanded to know what it was.

"It's a poinsettia, Soph. You know, a Christmas flower," Andrew said with a touch of big-brother superiority.

"Poynsetta? Poynsetta! Mizzetta Poynsetta!" Sophie cried, skipping about the room.

Jenny shook her head wearily. "I'm afraid we're going to miss the candlelight service this year because Maddie is still sick."

"No, no, you're not," Etta announced. "I'm here to baby-sit so you can all go. It's my Christmas present to the family."

Jenny was astonished. "But we can't accept. It's your very favorite service. You said yourself that you'd never miss it – even with a broken leg.'

"But this year I will, and gladly," the old lady replied, noticing with satisfaction that color was coming back to Jenny's tired face.

"Well, now. That's a true gift, Etta. I need to get out of the house. Thank you," Jenny said with renewed spirit. "Maddie's not contagious. You'll stay for supper, won't you? It's Maddie's favorite pea soup and she's getting her appetite back at last.

"Yes, I will," Etta replied. "And may I eat with her? She might like the company."

Jonathan, never one to talk much, carried a big tray of soup and cornbread up the steep old cape stairs while Etta bustled about the invalid's room, straightening books and dolls and bed covers. "There now. Everything's shipshape. Are you feeling better?"

Madeleine nodded. The seven year old was propped up in bed, several pillows newly fluffed behind her back. The long dark hair curling about her face emphasized how pale and thin she was, but her large eyes were radiant with new health. "What was Sophie calling you, Miss Etta?"

"That was so funny, my dear. Your mother gave me a beautiful poinsettia pin, and Sophie thought it rhymed. Mizzetta Poynsetta," she said.

"Mizzetta Poynsetta." – Maddie repeated the name several times in waltz-time until the elderly woman found herself whirling about the little room and she collapsed laughing into a chair.

* * *

Once the family had set off for church, the two friends could get down to serious business. "Now tell me about your childhood, Mizzetta," Maddie pleaded. It was their favorite pastime together.

"Well, now," the old woman said, folding her hands in her lap and contemplating them seriously. "Let me tell you about Christmas candlelight services when I was young. We tried to keep our candles lit all the way to our house. Bringing the Christmas spirit home, we called it. But sometimes it was tricky in the wind. One stormy night my friend Betsy brought a kerosene lamp chimney and put it right over her candle. Well, she got the flame home all right, but we knew it was cheating!"

"Let's have a candlelight service right here," the little girl suggested.

"Oh, Maddie, such a lovely idea!" Etta was galvanized into action. "Where does your mother keep the candles?"

"They're in the emergency box outside my bed- room door," Maddie explained.

The old lady was thankful she didn't have to brave those stairs more than once. "Here we are," she exclaimed, bringing back candles and holders and matches. "Your family is well prepared.'

"Now what do we do?" Maddie asked, climbing hurriedly out of bed.

"Put on your bathrobe first," Etta answered, mindful of the child's fragile health. Besides, she was stalling for time to think up a meaningful ritual.

The old woman turned out the bedroom lamp and struck a match. "Here, I light my candle," she explained, "and then you light yours from mine. I call this sharing the symbol of love." Maddie touched her wick to the flame. "And then – Etta was inspired – we sing happy birthday to Jesus!"

Maddie gasped. "We don't do that in church!" she giggled.

"Well, it's his birthday, isn't it? Next we sing Silent Night, and then we'll *hum* a verse." And so they did, thrilled by the candles' gleam reflecting in each other's eyes. The old woman would gladly have lingered in this spiritual vortex, but Maddie was eager to move on. "I want some Christmas cookies, Mizzetta. I smelled Mommy baking them this afternoon."

"Go ahead, then, but slowly," Etta admonished the child. "You may get dizzy not being out of bed in so long." Maddie giggled again. "I've been out of bed a lot since my fever broke. Don't tell."

After replacing the candles and matches safely in the emergency box, the elderly woman gingerly descended the stairs, holding firmly to the rails on either side.

"Wait! Wait!" Maddie called out from the kitchen. "I'm fixing a surprise."

Etta stood anxiously, a little alarmed by the rattles and bangs of preparation. "Okay – come in. I'm ready now!" Maddie's voice was a sing-song of excitement. When the old woman stepped into the kitchen, her surprise was real indeed. The kitchen table had been transformed with candles and a white tablecloth. It was almost like an altar, the old lady noticed, with two glasses of milk and a plate of her absolute most favorite Christmas sugar cookies – stars and trees with red and green sugar sprinkles. "Oh, my dear, it's perfect!" But Etta was no more delighted than Maddie herself. They sat down at opposite ends of the table, folded their hands and bowed their heads. "You do the blessing, Maddie," Etta said.

The little girl squeezed her eyes tight and took a deep breath, remembering her father's words: "Thank you, God, for all our blessings. Bring all the ships at sea safe home to harbor. And, uh ...give baby Jesus a birthday kiss and give us this day our daily... um ... *cookies.*" Her little hand was already half-way to the plate as she was saying "amen.*"

The old woman peered off into the living room at the glowing Christmas tree and sighed contentedly as she dipped a sugar star into her milk – just as she always had done as a young child – and nibbled a cold, sweet star-point.

"You're doing it like communion," aren't you?" Maddie noticed.

"Why, so I am!" the old woman exclaimed with a grin. In her head, Etta heard the lighthouse comment quite distinctly,

TWO! TWO!

"Yes, Al," she said to herself, "the message is crystal clear ... two are gathered here in His name."

"This is great, Mizzetta!" Maddie was in tune with Etta's thought. "We're not missing church at all. It's right here." Etta surprised herself with her own answer. "I'm so glad I came to see you, Maddie. It's the most perfect candlelight service I've ever been to – and being with you made it that way."

* * *

33

In the first hour of Christmas Morning, Etta was happily humming "Hark the Herald Angels Sing" as she traipsed about in her old flannel nightgown, completing her bedtime ritual of turning the heat down and brushing her teeth and opening the window a sliver. A cold blast of air swirled about her ankles, reminding her that the temperature had dropped twenty degrees during the evening.

She punched the pillow and squirmed under the comforter, exhausted, just as her orange Coon cat landed heavily beside her and demanded his place in the very center of the feather bed.

"Heave over, Keekah," the old woman said "You've got to give me a little room." She closed her eyes. "What a wonderful day I had. Thank you, God, for giving me this life and this day, for the sparkle in Maddie's eyes and the color in Jenny's cheeks – and for that crazy conversation with Owl's Head Light. It reminded me that it's *not* better to give than to receive. Giving and receiving are all one act and the gift is always doubled by sharing it."

She could have sworn that the lighthouse said spiritedly, softly …

TRUE! TRUE!

"Still expecting to have the last word, eh, Al?" Etta commented sleepily. "Your vocabulary is severely limited. Practice saying "verily, verily" instead," she sniffed.

* * *

Outside her window, stars as huge as pullet eggs glittered in the frosty Maine midnight. The surface of the tidal cove had frozen in thick sheets, but she hardly heard the cracking and moaning as the tide ebbed and flowed beneath the jagged, breaking ice.

Mizzetta Poynsetta was already fast asleep and blissfully searching for sugarplums.

XXX

THE CAT WHO
CAUGHT CHRISTMAS

THE CAT WHO CAUGHT CHRISTMAS

"... O'er the fields we go ... laughing all the way ... HO HO HO!" Etta's white hair flew in the electric-dry winter air. She punctuated the HO's with one hand as if conducting an orchestra, as her four-wheeler sailed through Thomaston and then swung sharp right onto Dexter Street, almost of its own accord. Half-humming, half-singing, body bouncing on the rutted road in rhythm with her music, she was suddenly embarrassed, glanced into the rear-view mirror hoping that no one had noticed her silliness. After all, she was on a serious Christmas mission. Her young neighbor, Jenny Morrill – mother of three active young children – had asked a favor of the elderly woman. "Find us a darling little kitty at the shelter. A Christmas present for the whole family – you'll know just which one is right for us."

Etta Leighton had agreed a bit too quickly. In truth, the shelter was a dangerous place for her. Every time she went there – even before she climbed their stairs and opened the door – she could hear the caged dogs yipping and a huge lump (so enormous and painful it almost prevented her speaking) would grow in her throat. The Knox County Animal Shelter has a policy never to put an animal down. Never. Soft-hearted animal lovers like Etta feel obliged to do everything they can to find homes for the homeless. "I'd like to take them all – every cat in the place!" Etta had often admitted to herself.

She waved to a couple of the teen-age volun-teers who groom and cuddle these lovely creatures. Then she walked directly to the kitten room and peered through the glass door. A dozen fluffy darlings were tumbling over each other, each one more adorable than the last. It was going to be a difficult choice! But Etta knew that a kitten would somehow choose itself, through a look or a cry or some "Take me, I'm yours" gesture. But first, Etta decided to check out the adult cat room. There, on several levels of shelf and climbing post, cats of every color sat and slept and stretched and meowed. Some were bedraggled and depressed, while others were anxious and active, showing how much they still loved life and needed to be loved. Tears pricked at the corners of Etta's eyes.

And then of course it happened, just as the old woman feared it would. Her roving gaze locked onto a huge ball of fur jammed into the corner of a cage by itself. It was a long-hair 'money cat," a tricolor with dark brown and white markings, patches of coin-shaped golden-orange especially around her face and a grimy white ruff. She could be a beauty but for those awful eyes! They were mere slits of fierce hostility.

"What's that one doing by herself?" Miss Etta asked Colleen Morang, the shelter's Volunteer Coordinator, who had come out of her office to say hello. "Oh, she's a mean one, Colleen explained. "Spits and lashes out at everyone. We call her "Hissyfit." She's maybe four years old. We've had her for over three months. The volunteers don't go near her. Good thing she's been de-clawed! You sure don't want that one, Etta.'

The elderly woman nodded and swallowed furtively, trying to manage the lump of pity in her throat. She unlatched the wire cage and reached toward Hissyfit with one finger – aiming straight for the spot between her lowered, half-closed eyes. Then an odd thing happened. The cat, surprised by the gentle touch, stretched up to receive it, and a deep, rumbling purr started in her throat. But suddenly the trapped animal recognized her own vulnerability. A fierce slash, and her clawless paw thrust aside Etta's hand. She hissed, spat, and retreated deeper into the corner of the cage.

"There! You see? She's wicked mean!" Colleen exclaimed unnecessarily.

"Okay, I'll take her," Etta replied instantly – all idea of cuddly kitten dashed by the short-lived purr of a venomous cat. Colleen shook her head, knowing better than to argue, and filled out the adoption papers.

* * *

Hissyfit was quickly dropped into the flowered pillowcase that was the widow's usual system for bringing home shelter cats. A twist and a tuck under her body kept the cat immobile on the front seat of Etta's car. It was not appreciated. "It's going to take a million years to think up a story for Jenny," Etta was thinking. "I'll just tell her I'll take Hissyfit if they don't want her. But I somehow think she's the right cat for them!"

Etta crossed the green bridge into Cushing and continued down River Road to Fales General Store. "Better fill up the gas tank," she decided, when she spotted the Morrills' car in the lot.

"Well, Hissyfit, I think you're going to your new home right now! Etta laid her hand on the lump she took to be a head, and Hissyfit squirmed in fear. The frantic feline answered with a muffled squeak that sounded like a Mainer's "Ehyuh." And Etta gave the cat a gentle squeeze of reassurance – which caused the opposite effect.

It all happened too fast. Young Andrew Morrill ran down the steps shouting "Hi, Mizzetta," and swung open the car door on the cat's side. The old woman exclaimed *"No! Don't!"*

just as Hissyfit gave a violent twist, uncoiled the pillowcase and dove for the dirt. Another instant and she had disappeared into the brush along the edge of Broad Cove.

"What was *that*?" Andrew asked in surprise.

Etta couldn't help laughing. "Just your family's Christmas present!" she said.

"Oooh, a kitty! Just what I want! How can we catch her?" Andrew, at 7, was old enough to know that a simple chase was bound to fail.

Let's talk to the Fales. They'll be able to help us," Etta replied.

The little store was filled with the Morrill clan -- eight year old Maddie with her dark eyes wide with interest, three-year-old Sophie posing in her newest birthday shirt, father Jonathan holding baby Olivia, while Jenny paid Richard Fales for their groceries and Elaine, Richard's wife, helped another customer.

Like all good general stores, Fales is a center for exchanging local concerns and sharing community information. Etta believes that the natural friendliness of Cushing probably began with the earliest Fales. It continues today. The family takes their position seriously; their unwritten rules are to stay neutral in any controversy and to be helpful to their customers – good Down East values, Etta calls them.

"Our kitty's down by the water," Andrew explained, "...and she doesn't know where she lives yet!" Everyone began talking at once. Richard raised a hand to get their attention. "First let's make a sign. We can tack it up for everyone to read." He pulled out a piece of paper and a marking pen and began to write as Andrew and Etta dictated:

LOST December 22
In front of Fales Store
Long hair money cat

42

"We don't have to explain that a money cat is an orange, brown and white female, do we?" Etta asked. "If we ever found a *male* cat with those three colors he'd be worth *real money!*" Everyone nodded silently. It was common knowledge that cat genes did odd things. Female tri-colors only give birth to female tri-colors, never males. In fact, they usually had marmalade orange males instead, so a three-colored male would be a prize indeed.

"How old is it?" Richard wanted to know.

"Oh, about four years old," Etta answered sheepishly.

Jenny sprang to attention. "Etta! Don't you mean four *months?*"

"There now, Jenny," the older woman said, looking her in the eye for the first time. "I'll explain about Hissyfit when we get to your house."

"Hissyfit? Oh my!" Jenny was clearly dismayed. She looked first at Jonathan, then at Elaine and last at Richard, but they were studying their shoes to keep themselves from chuckling out loud. Etta Leighton's reputation for rescuing stray cats was well known!

"One last thing, folks. I'll put some food and milk out to the barn. When she gets hungry, I'll catch her. Don't worry – I'm betting you'll have her back by Christmas Eve!"

So Etta handed the flowered cat-sack over to the Fales. As they traipsed single file out of the General Store, everyone was calling plaintively "Here, kitty, kitty," and searching the brush and watching the road for a terrified money cat.

* * *

Christmas Eve dawned cold and crisp and clear. Jonathan bundled everyone into boots and scarves and snowsuits. The Morrill children were off to Hathorne Point for their traditional Christmas ride in a real horse-drawn sleigh through the field below the Olson House. Their friends, John and Linda Duffy, own a Morgan horse named Sassafras who

43

loves to greet the tourists at the house in the summer, because they make a fuss over her and take her picture and sometimes feed her sandwiches. In the winter, when the Olson House is boarded up, she likes best to trot through the snow, steam blowing in huge clouds from her nostrils, sleigh bells jingling. Sassy seems to know that a special Christmas treat is sure to follow her good work.

Jonathan always takes the last ride, sitting very stern and still with the youngest child on his lap, holding tight as the wind whips his face and causes the tears to run down his cheeks.

"Daddy has a red nose!" Sophie laughed and pointed a mitten at him. "...and so does Olivia!"

"Come get your treat for Sassy, and be sure to hold your fingers out very, very flat so she won't nibble them!" Their father spoke so seldom that the children listened to every word. Sassy shuddered impatiently and pawed the frozen ground. Her favorite treat of the whole year was a red and white candy cane and today she would have *three* to munch. She ran her tongue over her teeth and blissfully licked her lips.

"Oooh, she loves them!" Maddie said, giving the Morgan a nose scratch. Sassy sniffed Maddie all over for more candy, running her muzzle along the snowsuit zipper until the little girl was paralyzed with giggles. "That's enough, Sassy," Linda, her owner, commanded. The horse snorted in disgust and backed away, sleigh and all, eyeing the children suspiciously. She wanted *more!*

"Time to go home now." Every year Jonathan said the same thing with exactly the same little shiver.

"Good-bye. Good-bye. Thank you, Sassy!" the children shouted as they piled into their car, flushed with cold and excitement – and oh so ready for home and cookies and hot chocolate.

* * *

Whoosh. Cold air swept into the house ahead of three laughing children. Olivia was waving her mitten and Sophie's eyes sparkled. "Mommy, Mommy! Sassy ate a candy cane right off my glove!" "She nibbled my zipper!" Maddie added. "And she takes the turns on one runner!" Andrew said, describing the dynamics of his ride in some detail, while Etta set out mugs of warm chocolate and a plateful of Christmas cookies shaped like stars and trees with red and green sprinkles thick on top.

"Is Hissyfit here?"

"Not yet, dear," Etta answered. "But she's on her way. That's why I'm here. Mr. Fales has caught her and he's bringing her to the house very soon now." The children ran through the house clapping and shouting "*Hurray Hissyfit!*" until Jenny carried the baby off for her nap, and Jonathan and Etta explained how quiet they would have to be so as not to frighten the new cat.

"Will she bite me?" Sophie asked.

"She's mostly scared," Etta said. Once she gets used to you, she'll be just fine. Do you think you can watch her and not chase her?" Sophie nodded solemnly.

Etta thought that Richard would've looked more like Santa with the sack slung over his back, but he came to the house with the struggling cat cradled tenderly in his arms. Every child had found a chair to sit in. "Shush!" they said a too little loudly. When he laid the wiggling cat-sack on the floor and opened it, out burst Hissyfit ready to fight, but all she found was quiet acceptance, and that gave her a dite of confidence. Within minutes the cat was slinking from room to room with her tail tight between her legs, edging along the walls, sniffing and glancing anxiously behind her.

"Nice cat," Richard said quietly. "Took only an hour for her to come running when I put some cat food out in the shed. Guess she could smell it all right. And she must've been hungry because I sneaked right up on her whilst she was eating."

"She looks scruffy, Etta, but I do believe she's mostly Maine Coon Cat," Jenny said with obvious approval. "She'll be a beauty once we fatten her up – look at those fluffy orange britches!

Sophie bounced off her chair, sending the panicky cat flying behind the sofa.

"Oops! I'm sorry, Hissy! I just want to get a cookie," the little girl explained.

It was a peaceful time in the Morrill house. The grown-ups chatted quietly about local happenings, and Jenny told everyone how Olivia had played the Christ Child in the church pageant. "She lay in the manger cooing and waving her rattle, like she was blessing everyone," her proud mother said. Should have had a big sign saying "It's a girl," Etta commented dryly, but Jonathan and Richard only gave each other knowing looks and no one laughed out loud. Etta liked to make feminist jokes.

The new cat continued to explore the whole house, upstairs and down. "Look," Etta said, "She's already carrying her tail straight out behind her. I think she's beginning to like this place."

The money cat marched purposefully past the lighted Christmas tree toward the window seat and hopped up next to Jenny's enormous geranium plant, the one that's been growing bigger and bushier every year. Christmas-red blooms glowed wherever the sun shone through them. The cat leaned over for a sniff. Her ears perked and her body arched intently. "what's she doing?" Maddie whispered. "Shh, let's watch," Jenny whispered back.

Hissy closed her eyes as she inhaled the odd fragrance, then tipped her head and looked out the window. "I believe she's remembering,' Richard explained. "Something in her past is coming back to her."

The cat hopped down from the window seat and looked him in the eye. "Ehyuh," she squeaked. It was unnerving, as if she truly understood what he had said.

46

"Oh, oh! That voice sounds like she's caught a cold," Jonathan noticed.

They observed quietly, as the cat continued to come back to life. Carrying her tail like a triumphant flag, she sauntered over to the Christmas tree and rose slowly on her hind legs. Ever so gracefully with both paws she grasped a large silver ball -- Jenny's favorite decoration, the one painted with the nativity scene of Mary, Joseph, the Babe in the manger and the Star of Bethlehem.

"Well, I never! It looks like she's caught Christmas!" Etta said. As she spoke, the cat patted the ball gently and, with tail high, strolled off to the parents' bedroom, where she stretched out on Jenny's hand-made quilt and fell into an exhausted sleep.

"That's funny," Andrew commented. "Now we can't call her Hissy because she doesn't hiss anymore. Maybe we should call her *Christmas*."

Jenny had been thinking about a new name too. "Let's call her Christina, after Christmas and Christina Olson, who loved geraniums, too. I think her name is Miss Chris."

Richard nodded. "Good name, and, if I remember rightly, Christina loved cats too." Everyone agreed the name was perfect.

"We're keeping her, right? Maddie asked.

"Of course, dear," her mother answered. "Miss Chris is our gift to the whole family. We knew Miss Etta would find us the right one," and she looked at Etta with a knowing grin.

"Now we have Mizzetta Poinsetta and Miss Chris too!" Maddie exclaimed. "We're a lucky family."

Miss Etta touched the poinsettia pin the Morrills had given her last Christmas. It was the reason why they sometimes called her "Mizzetta Poinsetta" now

Etta was thinking how curious it was that things usually work out for the best. A feisty cat nobody wanted had found her home at last, and it was Etta's privilege to help make it all happen. *Thank you for cats,* she said under her breath. *Thank you for my life. And thank you for the love and respect that fills this little house. I do believe the spirit of Christmas is here all year long.*

"Oh, it's much more than luck," she said out loud, looking around the room at all the serene and happy faces. "Wouldn't you say that we're very blessed indeed?"

Miss Chris didn't need to answer such a self-evident question any more than the family did. She merely sighed a long, contented sigh and stretched luxuriously on the warm quilt. Was she dreaming about her first mistress, who grew geraniums like Jenny's? She rolled over onto her back and trustingly exposed her tummy – a cat's sure sign that she feels secure in her home.

It's doubtful that she woke at all from her peaceful sleep on that Christmas Eve in Cushing.

XXX

ABOUT MISS CHRIS

The basics of this story are true. The author found a frightened Hissyfit at the Shelter and took her home in 1997 – convinced by that single purr that the cat was merely terrified, rather than mean. She slept for twelve hours straight that first night. Once having inhaled the essence of geraniums she was forever redeemed, and treated the Christmas tree with the simple reverence described in the story.

Now she's ten pounds heavier, cleans herself to a fluffy shine and often walks with her tail straight up in Maine Coon fashion. Miss Chris has several important household duties – fetching a mouse, cuffing a younger cat into proper behavior, meditating on the deck on sunny mornings, avoiding the snow, observing the tides of Maple Juice Cove, daintily eating some morsel of food, balancing on her hind legs, rolling in the sun-warmed gravel of the driveway, and smelling the flowers.

* * *

THE SERENE SEASON

THE *Serene Season*
AN ALLEGORY

"Bert, don't play games! Come along!" Agnes called sharply to her son. She scurried along the edge of Pleasant Point Road, keeping well into the grasses, slipping on the wet snow, listening all the while for any faint rustlings in the bushes. There he was at last, peering through the stiff brown weed-stalks, grin turning to grimace as he limped toward her.

"Berty," her voice squeaked with concern, "what's happened to you?"

"It's nothing, Mamma – I'm okay."

Agnes knew better. "You've been up to Dr. Benson's old place," she scolded.

Bert ducked his head in disgrace. "Well, I wanted to see how many cats live there now. I was being real careful, hiding in the rocks under the barn, when the big gray one pounced outta nowhere. Oh, Mamma, what awful teeth! The lady ran out of the house and grabbed that ole cat by the neck and shook it and it let go and I didn't know if I should run or play dead ..." (Bert was running out of breath) "and the lady yelled at me *Go, silly chipmunk* ... and I *went!*"

As an afterthought he added, "It doesn't hurt much, honest."

Agnes stroked her paws expertly over his hind leg, deciding he was more bruised than damaged. She shook her head helplessly in the face of adolescent immortality, and said a little prayer of thanks for the human – a Cushinger, the mother called her – that saved his life. "Come along, then. You can carry the food."

In the old days, every root cellar in Cushing was brimful against the winter and every barn a treasure trove for wily rodents. Yesterday they had picked up a bit of food at the Grange, stuff they'd squirreled away after the Halloween party. It wasn't much, but enough to share.

Bert disappeared. Several small animals hurried past her, headed in the same direction, chattering "Hello, hello, see you at the church." Agnes turned onto Salt Pond Road, her spirits lifting in anticipation of old friends to greet, gossip and stories to exchange. Every year it was the same. A tradition. The animals gathered in the old church to worship their Creator on this night – the same night Cushingers call Christmas.

The sky was a wash of mauve softening to gray. Ahead she could barely make out the shadows of two old friends plodding along the side of the road. "Hey, wait for me," she called, and the two stopped and turned.

The old porcupine was scruffier than she re-membered him, and grayer around the eyes, but he greeted her with a flourish of his walking cane, just like always. "Agnes, Serene Season to you!"

"Uncle John, you're a welcome sight." He bent down for her to give him a peck on the cheek. Agnes turned to his partner. "Fay, I do believe you're flourishing! Where have you been keeping yourself?" The Raccoon too leaned down so they could rub cheeks. Agnes was a tiny presence between these two giants.

Fay grinned. "You won't believe where I spent the summer! I had a penthouse in the Olson House chimney. No elevator, but such a spectacular view – Monhegan Island in fair weather. One night when they were closing up, I made too much noise and they thought Christina's ghost was upstairs." The three old friends laughed merrily. "Cushingers don't know much about the real world around 'em," Uncle John remarked, chewing on the piece of straw he always kept stuck between his teeth.

"And the saddest thing," Fay continued: "A new neighbor has built a gigantic barn next door. "It's out of keeping -- destroys the lonely severity of the place. Now, you can't even see the water view from the third floor where that artist used to paint.

Uncle John shook his head glumly. "People from away come to Maine for the simple life, but there's something' in 'em that can't help makin' poor choices."Don't seem to know nuthin' 'bout bein' good neighbors. Some of 'em, anyways," John corrected himself.

He chewed and thought for a while. "...and they don't seem to know the land ahn't really theirs – they just get to tend it for a while." The three friends nodded, sighed, reliving the centuries-old sadness of Cushingers encroaching on their beloved woodlands. A sudden chill breeze swept across Maple Juice Cove, striking at the back of their necks and causing the fur to rise.

* * *

Mamma, Mamma, come quick!" Bert was scampering toward the three, knapsack straight out behind him as he rushed headlong down the hill. "Something's wrong with our church!" The three hurried forward. Above them, seabirds were circling noiselessly, as if a storm were approaching. Many small country animals crouched in stunned silence along the road's edge, staring up the hill toward their destination, the little white church on the hill.

What met their gaze was totally unexpected – a true shock. The spire was gone! Plucked from its proud pedestal, it stood pathetically on the ground. The front wall had been stripped bare of planking. In its place were sheets of black under-sheathing nailed on with lath, and a tall scaffolding of pipes and wood. It appeared dark and ominous. The faces of the little animals reflected their dismay.

Pastor Leonard, perched on the signpost, ruffled his black feathers against the wind. The sign beneath his tail was weathered but legible:

1854
SOUTH CUSHING
BAPTIST CHURCH

The old crow cleared his throat several times. As spiritual leader, it was surely his duty to comment on the horror and calm the crowd. But what could he say? What was the truth?

* * *

For a hundred and forty four years the church had stood serenely on its hill, self-assured, contented, satisfied with itself despite outward appearances. It had been erected on a bald knoll, without a tree to soften its outline. By 1854 every trunk and bough had already been chopped down by Cushingers who scavenged the wood to heat stoves, to build houses, to feed the limekilns and to clear the fields for planting.

Once the church had been a place of worship, filled with people singing and pastors spouting fire-and-brimstone. But times changed and trees sprang up around it, a more fitting backdrop for its spare simplicity. Then it was all but abandoned. Finally it was deeded to the Cushing Historical Society to preserve it in the best way they could. They still hold an annual church service every summer, just as the Baptists had required when they signed the building over. And they have promised never to modernize the original 1854 building with electricity or running water.

A few weddings every year have given it a semblance of purpose, but Maine weather is hard on its buildings. The pointed steeple angled to the side a little more each year, the ceiling drooped, the floor sagged, the paint chalked from harsh salt winds. At one point it was suggested, *seriously suggested*, that the church be sold or torn down. The animals too were sadly aware that their little church was decaying around them, but they were powerless to prevent its demise.

* * *

"What's happening here, Pastor?" Someone cried out.

"Caw!" The Pastor cleared his throat again and explained in a confident tone that belied his under-standing. "The church is molting." As a bird, he knew all about such things. But Berty had other thoughts. He had noticed a second and newer spire wrapped in swaddling cloths against the elements, lying on the ground. "Don't think so, Pastor," the little chipmunk said respectfully. "There are TWO spires now. I think it's *multiplying!*" (Any very young rodent knew all about such things.)

An audible gasp of disbelief and amazement rose from the gathering of animals. Over their heads the sea gulls burst into raucous laughter. "They're restoring the church," they cried, their voices screaming on the word 'restore.' "History is important to Cushingers. They care for this place as much as we do!"

And that was the simple truth of it.

* * *

The animals traipsed single-file along the edge of the trees, so Cushingers wouldn't see their many tracks and become too curious. The lowest planks of the church walls had not yet been replaced, but a sheet of thick, clear plastic acted as temporary protection against the winter weather. Uncle John propped up the edge with a stick so latecomers

57

could enter, and helped the tiny animals to craw under in single file. It was growing dark. The pews, unscrewed from the floor, were randomly scattered about the hall and a thick drift of sawdust covered everything in sight.

The old porcupine wandered about, tapping with his cane, checking the new construction. He discovered beams in the vestibule designed to support the new spire safe and upright. "Forever more," Uncle John muttered, satisfied at last. "No more holes in the foundation," he announced. "My cousins won't be living in the basement."

"No holes? How will we get in for the service next year?" Pastor Crow was distressed.

"Don't worry, Leonard," Uncle John reassured him. "Plans are already being made for a way in that no Cushinger will ever suspect. Ehyuh, everything's shipshape," he announced.

"Just look here." He pointed with his cane toward the ceiling. "No sag!" He jumped up and down on the floor. "No wobble!"

A mistake, that! All of the youngsters – chip-munks, squirrels, rabbits, skunks, even goldfinches and turtles – instantly forgot where they were and began to jump up and down in perfect rhythm. "No wobble! No wobble!" they shrieked in unison, lining up behind Pied Piper Porcupine and winding under the pews, around and about, little paws pounding. What a joyful parade! Mothers watched the harmless fun and wisely cheered them on, so the children calmed down soon enough, but Uncle John slumped under a pew, panting.

Pastor Leonard was first to notice another major improvement. The red velvet curtain that once covered the altar window had been pulled down and the ugly cement-block chimney that hid the view outside had been hauled away. "Ah!" Pastor Len exclaimed, "See how God's creation is framed!" Indeed, the tall window displayed a perfect picture: His evergreens starkly silhouetted against the last of

His sunset as the faintest pink touched the furred and feathered faces of His myriad creatures.

The animals settled down -- under their favorite pews or on them. The birds hastened to perch on the pew backs and the old upright piano. The hanging chandelier designed to hold Cushinger kerosene lanterns swung wildly and the glass prisms jingled like wind chimes, as the littlest birds jostled each other on its outstretched arms.

The Winter Bird Choir gathered in tens and twenties on the old oak chairs at the back of the hall (the very same chairs the Baroquen Consort (a group of recorder-playing Cushingers) use when they play for the annual church service in August). These singers tried in every way to atone for the fact that the true songbirds had gone South and weren't due back until May. They made up in vigor what they lacked in vibrato, and someone commented kindly that perhaps the crows simply didn't have the tunes memorized yet.

Several remarked afterwards that Pastor Leonard gave a fine sermon. The theme was Universal Love, but Berty wasn't sure how well that worked out in the real woodland world. Halfway through the sermon, the young chipmunk needed to relieve himself. "Go outside, Dear," Agnes said, pointing to the propped-up plastic door." We don't soil the church."

"But it's dangerous out there!" Bert answered, wide-eyed, imagining the burnished teeth of fox and fisher and ferret – not to mention horned owls and things that go bump in the night. "Tonight is safe. It's the Serene Season," Agnes assured him. "All the great beasts promise a day of abstention, out of respect."

He trusted his mother, and Uncle John nodded agreement, so Berty ducked under the plastic and out into the crisp night air.

The tiny chipmunk's heart slammed in his chest. "I'm imagining this!" he thought, terror and awe awash in his body. "It's not possible!"

All the great beasts of the forest had come. They stood worshipfully in the thin layer of snow well behind the church (so as not to be seen in Cushinger headlights) Moose and deer abided quietly between the trees, fox and coyote among the bushes, horned owls and hawks in the branches. But fishers and ferrets slipped stealthily hither and thither among them. "No, no! Not to be trusted," Bert thought, "No matter what they say."

One of the foxes greeted him without the slightest hint of slyness in his voice. "Serene Season to you, Bert. From out here, the Choir sounds pretty good, all things considerin'."

The young chipmunk nodded briefly and smiled with an effort, did his business and scurried back to the protection of the church. Fay the Raccoon was at the podium, just finishing her predictions for '99. She was a first-class fortuneteller and this was the highlight of the service.

"...and this little church will be restored," she was saying. "This coming summer, the Historical Society will have an elegant art show and make enough money to complete the repairs."

(*"What is money?"* Bert whispered. "Shhh," his mother answered.)

"A huge motor crane will lift the new steeple high, and place it safely *there*." Fay pointed triumphantly to the ceiling and the sky beyond. " ... and Cushingers will come to cheer.

(*"Can we come too?"*) Bert whispered so insistently that finally Agnes nodded.

Fay concluded with a flip of her ringed tail, in an odd sing-song voice, "They'll paint the church you see – it will glisten white as can be – here on the hill in the sun – for years and years to come."

60

"Years and years and years," whispered hundreds of sleepy children, curling comfortably against their mothers, their heads tucked under their arms.

"May the Serene Season bless you all," Pastor Leonard concluded.

"Bless us all," the congregation replied.

Agnes squeezed Bert's paw. Uncle John was already snoring softly beside her, but Bert listened to the soft shuffling outside as the great beasts withdrew. And the deep contentment of the little church enfolded him. "For years ... and ... years ... to ... come," he repeated as his eyes slowly closed.

And so it came to pass.

FINIS

A Sense of Community

In 1997, the Historical Society voted to restore the South Cushing Baptist Church. The vote was not unanimous. Some believed it was impossible to raise the necessary monies, and recommended instead that we sell the building or tear it down.

Indeed, it was a huge undertaking for such a small population. The Society itself has some 225 members. The midcoast Maine town of Cushing has a winter population of only 1,200 souls that swells to 1,800 when the summer residents arrive.

The majority prevailed. A three-year pledge program was mailed to every resident in Town. It reached its goal, but then more serious, but hidden structural damage was uncovered. By the winter of '98 funds were exhausted and repairs had ceased.

A wave of renewed energy resulted in a second mailing, and the sale of stylish T-shirts designed by a local artist. Cultural programs held in the church focused attention on the need and brought further contributions. In fact, the Society plans ongoing programs into the foreseeable future so that the church may continue to enjoy the attention and activity it deserves. Weddings are a mainstay of the church's activities.

Cushing artisans and artists were invited to participate in an art show and sale in the summer of '99 – an outstanding social, cultural and financial success. The Society reported sufficient funds to complete restoration and enough more to begin a satisfactory endowment fund. The total acquired by the Church Fund to date is more than $57,000, an astonishing measure of commitment!

The Serene Season is an allegory. I wanted to convey a sense of community. Like the animals portrayed, the very diverse people of Cushing gathered together for a common purpose and offered their many skills for the common good.

The feeling has been as spiritual in its own way as the reverence felt by the animals in the church on that fictitious serene night. We have preserved a piece of our common history – whether we came from away or were born to this soil – and we share in the knowledge that the little church on the hill is a symbol, both of our past and our future, and will continue to stand for years and years to come.

* * *

On November 4th, 1999 (which is also my brother "Uncle John's" birthday), the new steeple was swung up to its pedestal on the roof of the little church. How we cheered! Then at long last the weathervane, a simple verdigris-copper banner, was set at spire-point where it shifts now in the wind, it's slightest movement catching your eye, and drawing your attention skyward.

X X X

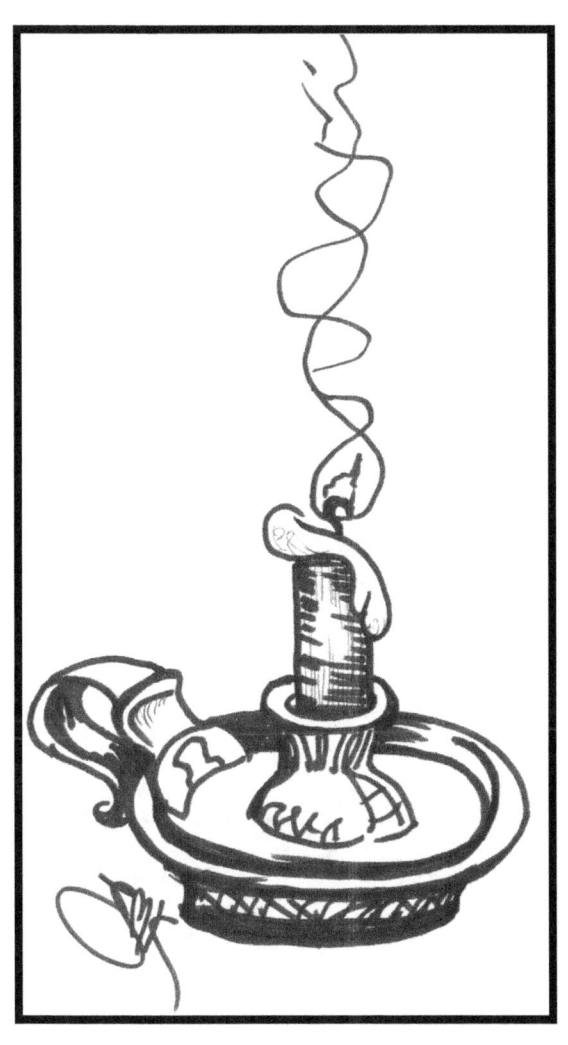

JUST WHERE DOES
CUSHING BEGIN?

JUST WHERE DOES CUSHING BEGIN?

Mainers know when someone is "from away." It means that they concede your right to be here while mindful of your lack of Maine roots. Arriving here, I wanted to shout "I'd have been born here if only my parents had the good sense to turn north from Massachusetts when they married, instead of trekking south to New Jersey." But of course explanations aren't necessary. I'm from away, here to stay – called by some magical force that tore me willingly from my old life and transplanted me joyfully in Cushing.

"And just what is Cushing?" you may inquire. During this holiday season, I've been asking myself that very question, because I was a stranger, and have come to feel welcome and accepted in this simple, peaceful place. Let me try to explain.

This tiny village, bordered by the St. George and Meduncook Rivers, sprawls across a granite and green peninsula stretching more than ten miles toward the cold green waters of the Atlantic Ocean. River Road begins at the Thomaston Bridge that spans the St. George, then lazily meanders toward the Gut, passing old capes and trailers, farmhouses and ponds, sheep and horses, meadows and fields, evergreen woods and distant glimpses of river and bay – all comfortably spaced out with room enough to breathe. Dirt fire-roads lead to year 'round homes and summer cottages, nestled in the woods or gracing the edge of the St. George. Some dwellings nearer the Point face on deep water and are unquestionably elegant.

Fales Store, about 6 miles from the Thomaston Bridge, is a focal point of Cushing, and its most meaningful exchanges are community information and concerns and simple small town friendliness. The owners, in a very real sense I believe, both set *and* reflect the tone of the town.

If you keep going straight at the store you soon come upon our Firehouse and Community School. Angling back toward Pleasant Point Road on the shortcut sits our pocket-handkerchief of a library.

So that's the center of town? Not exactly. Renee Vinal, the tax collector, has an office in her home way north of Fales about 3 miles up River Road, where she also sells lobsters. The Fire Warden has his official sign at his lane in North Cushing too but my next-door neighbor Norma Gardner is the Town Clerk, and she's two miles south of the general store.

The long road to the Gut changes its name from River Road to Pleasant Point as it turns just after Fales. Beyond the library shortcut is our little community church – a simple building with a short, square steeple, deep green shutters and that indescribable aura of resolute Maine spirit. A mile or so further you come upon Acorn Grange Hall, which has welcomed its members for a hundred years or so. Then comes the Post Office, and it's only a half-mile more to my home and then Norma's Town Clerk sign. So there's no real "center" to Cushing; it's more of a scattering of buildings and people. Probably the very fact that it's so spread out adds to the tranquility of the place.

It takes another few miles for Pleasant Point Road to dwindle into a delta of paths and the last homes on the Point. Here are a gathering of sailboats and lobster boats and good salt water. At the Gut, people can cross the flats to Gay Island when "mudzin" at low tide. Finally, a large sign proclaims "TOWNSEND," and so it is, but the truth is that the Townsends live there.

68

And the people themselves? Just like anywhere else, I suppose, but I think they have that special Maine attitude – neighborly willingness to mind their own business and yet offer real help whenever they are asked. It's a delightful mix of young and old, from away and native born. Cushing is an artists' community, a lobstering community, a young family community, a retirement community and much, much more. We usually have time to stop and chat while picking up provisions at Fales or buying stamps at the post office. In fact, the slow pace allows for at least a nodding acquaintance with any number of Cushingers. (I'm not sure that's quite the right term. Usually we just "live in Cushin'.")

From the green bridge to the gut, this road is a feast for the soul any time of year. Sometimes it's the lightest lemon-lime of hackmatack needles bursting forth in spring; or a field bountiful with proud stalks of lupine. It can be blue heron feeding or osprey diving and seagulls wheeling above the cove. Then again, it may be a snaking line of low flames glowing at dusk on meadows being burned off – or deepest fog rolling in from Broad Cove, muffling the distant double-toot of Owl's Head Light. It may be a towering pile of neon-painted lobster buoys, or a thanksgiving of earthy yellow fields scattered with fresh hay bales. It's searching the Milky Way on a moonless night, praying for northern lights and hearing, ominous in the distance, the victorious yip-yip of cat-craving coyotes. And it's glimpsing the quick flash of fox or deer in the brush, or swerving to avoid that slow-waddling porcupine or – the glory of it! – observing a moose observing *you*.

Sometimes the Fall leaves are so vibrant in the sun that they truly hurt my eyes, and the woodstove smoke smells sweet as it spreads level above the pines. In the sharp winds of winter, I'm bewitched by the groans of ice floes lifting and falling on the tides of Maple Juice Cove, and blinded by snowdrifts in the winter sun just after a blizzard.

No wonder this is a place where people share: "I feel so blessed to be here," and "How I love Cushing!"

* * *

Visual pleasures and gentle people are only part of the story. One day my son mentioned that there's a line on River Road where Cushing *really* begins – where the sense of serenity and security first rise to a conscious level. He said that it shifts a little from day to day, but it's obvious if you're alert to the subtle stirrings of your heart.

I took him seriously. The next time crossing the green bridge and heading for home, I paid special attention – skepticism mixing with anticipation – because something told me that it was true and I'd soon know it for myself.

My car passed the official town line at Matson's Lumber Yard, but nothing stirred. Realizing I was too tense, I took several deep breathes and relaxed as my car swung by Spear Mill Road and the sheep farm. I caught a glimpse of Hyler Cove and continued on, questioning myself repeatedly. "Do I feel different? Is this it?" Silly, I know, but there I was, entirely engrossed in the process.

My car came over a small hill. Nothing much lay in view but more road and woods, so the distinct change was startling as calm and comfort spread quietly through me. It was eerie. And yet somewhere beneath my conscious memory I always knew that the shift in feeling begins *there* for me, just as I pass the gazebo.

"Yes," my son confirmed, "right there. Quite powerful too at times." We smiled into each other's eyes and nodded in happy agreement. It was an oddly satisfying moment.

* * *

I couldn't let go of the idea, and soon found myself undertaking a marvelously unscientific experiment. I asked seven more people where Cushing starts for them -- 5 Mainers and 2 more that are surely "here to stay" – a total of nine in the sample. (I must admit they all live at Fales Store or south of it.) It pleased me that every one of them took my question seriously and didn't stare at me as if I were a bubble or two off level.

I asked my good friend Linda Duffy first. "Why, it's right *here*," she said as the car we were riding in together crested the little hill and passed the gazebo. "Never any question. I'm not at all surprised that we notice the same spot. It's the spirit of this place."

My friend and neighbor, Shirley Stenberg, had a similar answer, and she too said she has never tired of the pleasures of the delightful long drive home from the Thomaston bridge.

I had told Elaine Fales, owner of the general store, how much I hated to go shopping, and she answered that she didn't even like to leave Cushing. For five years I've been saying the very same thing. I don't like to cross the green bridge! So that was my opening, and her answer was telling. "It starts just as soon as I cross the bridge," she explained, "and gets stronger when I begin to smell good fresh air." She thought the gazebo was about the right line.

But David Provost (it's just my opinion that he's Cushing's best carpenter) explained that it surely begins at the sheep farm, "because you can get a first glimpse of water in the distance."

This was later confirmed by Richard Fales, Elaine's husband. "At Spear Mill Road," he said firmly. (The road takes a sharp curve around the sheep farm, a classic big-house-little-house-back-house-barn, and then heads more-or-less straight for his store.) He, thinking the gazebo-line was a bit too far from the bridge, suggested that I reacted to that spot because I live a couple of miles further south than

71

he does.

Brad Beckett, our local Cushing historian, pondered only a moment. "Why, it's just before Luthera's house," he said with conviction.

Which led me to Luthera Dawson. I delight in her wry wit and friendship. She lives in Thomaston now but grew up on a marvelous salt-water farm in Cushing in the 20's. Not surprisingly, the lane to her farm is a quarter-mile past the gazebo. Her answer was succinct. "I always had a strong feeling right there," she said, "but I thought it was because I was almost home."

By this time, you may well be thinking, "I know how much you love Cushing, but what does all this feeling-of-the-place stuff have to do with me ... and the holidays?"

Well, Luthera put her finger squarely on it. Cushing is another name for *home*.

XXX

*O*nce again my front door happily displays one of Jeannette Chapman's full and fragrant Christmas wreathes. I've made it a holiday tradition to be at the Church Fair just as the doors open in order to buy one – they vanish about as quickly as her doughnut holes!

And once again the windows of Cushing gleam with Christmas candles. I sketched the cover of this booklet as a reminder that the candle in the window is a beacon announcing to strangers and friends alike that we share with everyone the peace and love of the season.

* * *

I wish you the most serene of holidays and all the blessings of your own sense of 'home." It's not a town or a house, although it may be nurtured there. It's that place deep inside where trust and love enfold you, whether you live alone, with family or friends, or even with strangers.

May the light of welcome and acceptance shine ever brighter – *from* each of us and *to* each of us – throughout the coming year.

* * *

CREATURES WITH LONG GREEN TAILS

CREATURES WITH
LONG GREEN TAILS

This is a Holiday story about cats. Again. If you
don't revel in cats, I'm truly sorry, but here goes anyway . . .

Last year, Monty disappeared. He was huge, orange,
long-haired, loving -- and fluffy rather than fat, so I doubt a
Fisher got him. About that time someone spotted a Canadian
Bobcat near my home crossing the road toward Maple Juice
Cove. I suppose that could be the culprit, but I'm betting on
coyotes. Cushing Coyotes are clever. Sometimes I hear
them yipping over on Fresh Pond where they have their den.
Every few months the "Lost Cat" signs proliferate on Fales'
bulletin board (that's the Cushing General Store) and it's
certain they're prowling the area. Ah well – as my son says –
cats are born to break your heart.
It's my habit to rescue older cats from the local
Shelter, and I've had some characters. Older cats are
grateful to be rescued. They sprawl on the quilt, recognizing
true comfort, and smile secretly. They fatten up and purr and
never stray far – especially females. Monty, of course, was a
Tomcat who loved to tour the property and far beyond.
Sometimes it took him a day or more to return and I was
always heartsick and panic-stricken when that happened.
Yuma Cat and Madam, two middle-aged females,
were all that remained. It seemed reasonable to get a third
right away (It's not easy to control a cat-compulsion) so

within a few days I was off to the Shelter to find a grateful senior cat. I wasn't going for a kitten. Monty had been a kitten. Perhaps that's why he was so special, I'd nursed him back to health from near starvation and he'd grown up with me.

I didn't want another kitten.

Kittens, male or female, have little sense and they need nine lives because they insist on exploring in dangerous places. They *bounce*. They skitter the scatter rugs into bunches. I had no intention of even <u>looking</u> at the kittens. The Shelter has lots.

To get your own special cat, it's important to take time. I sat on the floor in the kitten room and waited for them to explore. One little Tuxedo cat (mostly black with two white dots under her nose like a mustache that made her look like a Charlie Chaplin photo negative) marched upon me and scrunched into a ball in my lap, purring blissfully. Instant adoration.

"The tricolor in the corner is her sister," the volunteer said helpfully (and hopefully.) Another person offered the same information. Would I break them up? Surely not!

"Okay, I'll take them both," I said, knowing that trouble had already brewed.

Naming these little demons (excuse me: little darlings) was easy. The Tuxedo cat is Lillybit – because she's just a lillybittacat to this day. Her sister the money cat, quite a bit bigger, presses her face to your neck and squirms with affection. She is Nuzzle. They tumbled and pounced and grew as kittens do and gave me much pleasure. Absolutely nothing lifts my spirit like the antics of two joyful kittens!

And then Lilly and Nuzzle reached puberty.

Lilly's natural instincts rose in her feline breast. "I can catch mice," she whispered at first, slipping through the cat door, her meow muted by a mouthful of brown fur. "I can bring them to you *live.*" She mentioned proudly, meows punctuated by frightened squeaks. She stalked them in the field, "Every Day!" She yowled.

And so it has been.

Lilly is a Master Mouser. She tosses her catch in the air, and rolls on top of the poor terrified thing in ecstasy. When one escapes and scurries for a closet, she is mortified. As a cat lover, I accept this predatory skill and praise the giver before catching the newest prize in a towel and letting it go out the door or putting it (sadly) in the special gift receptacle in the kitchen "Oh, good Lilly. What a wonderful cat!" (Stroke. Purr.)

Nuzzle was slower to mature. She observed Lilly's every move and sniffed at the gifts. She seemed puzzled but willing to learn. Thinking, studying, practicing, she eventually developed a hunting skill of astonishing originality.

"I can catch monsters," she whispered at first, slipping through the cat door, her meow muted by a mouthful of brown grass. "I can bring them to you live," she mentioned proudly, meows punctuated by long swinging tails. Sometimes she had difficulty maneuvering the huge monsters, tipping her head sideways to stuff everything through the cat door. She chased them across the lawn, "Every Day!" She yowled.

And so it has been ever since.

Nuzzle is a Master at Monsters. She tosses her catch in the air, and rolls on the poor chewed thing in ecstasy. After the lawn is freshly mowed, she brings a huge mouthful of cut grass to me and I spread it apart gently, searching for creatures inside. They are usually wet and torn and bitten, and absolutely never escape her. Only their long green tails quiver when she drops them at my feet. "Oh, good Nuzzle, what a wonderful cat." (Stroke. Purr.)

And just what are these green-tailed beasts?

Whether they be large or small –
They're only leaves, after all.

Spiritually speaking, Nuzzle is a Vegetarian.

I share this absolutely true little story with you because it is delightful and humorous and we need delight and humor this year of all years. Their kitten-gifts remind me of the true meaning of Christmas. The value of any gift comes from the love and intent of the giver. Nuzzle's monster-leaf with the quivering green tail is just as freely offered as Lilly's scurrying mouse (and easier to catch and clean up after!) Their pride is equally strong and their ecstasy contagious. These offerings come from the very core of their cat-creation – and I receive their gifts and appreciate them with that understanding clearly in mind.

Think of this tiny book as my own green leaf. This year in particular, imagine that it is wrapped in everlasting peace.

May the year 2002 usher in a new beginning for this weary world. May we reach deep within and find peace like a green, growing leaf in our hearts.

THE GIFT IN
GAMMA'S GARDEN

TO HONOR AND REMEMBER
MY GRANDMOTHER

BERTHA LEIGHTON JACKSON

1879 · 1973

&

THE *GIFT* IN
GAMMA'S GARDEN

To me, she was quite perfect. By most measures, however, she was a simple, ordinary woman, and she and my mother had many strong differences. That said, the overriding truth is that she loved me and I, her eldest granddaughter, loved her just as deeply.

Meeting a friend's very tall grandmother for the first time, I reasoned, "That's not a *real* Gammy!" A real one is short and cuddly and wears glasses with gold wire earpieces and no rims. She struggles into corsets with stiff stays and changes clothes two, maybe three times a day. And she doesn't need a car; because the trolley rattles by every half hour, at the bottom of the hill on the outskirts of Worcester,

Massachusetts. (My hometown in New Jersey had no trolleys by then, but a trace of old tracks still peeked through the asphalt around the town square.)

Gamma grew up just outside of Boston and spoke with that wonderful New England accent that so mystified me as a child. "What a good *idear*. Let's do it, *Deah*!" she'd say to me with genuine enthusiasm, and we'd head out on some trolley-bound adventure. Or she might mention my cousin "Mather." Some time later, I learned my cousin spelled her name M-a-r-t-h-a.

During the early forties, I spent six weeks each summer with my grandparents. My father shook his head in mock despair: "It takes six full weeks to straighten her out again once she comes home," he'd say to my mother with a grin. What could he mean? After all, I was perfectly behaved at Gamma's – and we always did just exactly what I wanted to do!

They lived very modestly. Gampa was a clerk at Washburn's Plumbing and Hardware in the center of Worcester. He was a true New England man, seldom talking, always tinkering. He rode an early trolley to work, so Gammy was up at five sharp to make him breakfast – usually oatmeal or shredded wheat and fruit – and he never _ever_ forgot to kiss Gamma goodbye. Each summer workday he left us "girls" to do chores that were distinctly foreign to this suburban New Jersey seven year old.

They lived in a time warp.

Not an easier time, surely, but simpler. My job was to chop the last of the ice in the icebox with a wood-handled ice pick, pushing it aside to make way for the new block. I turned the big orange card in the window from the side marked NO to the side requesting ICE. Within hours a horse-drawn cart pulled up outside, and Iceman Jim climbed down, wearing a red rubber cape strapped to his back. Setting wrought iron tongs deep into a slippery block, bending his knees and reaching behind him, Jim leaned forward to settle the ice against his upper back. On the hottest August days, ice-melt rolled down the rubber into a catch strip sewn along the bottom of the cape, just as Jim's bandana caught the rolling sweat from his forehead. With a grunt, he swung the huge block into the top of the icebox and dropped the oak lid with an echoless *thud.* Then he chatted for a while with Gammy before proceeding with his deliveries. It was a satisfying routine, this friendly giant come to visit the fairy Godmother.

And we were always busy!

I helped with the cooking. Two pots with beans, water, brown sugar and spices, topped with squares of salt pork, were lowered into the "slow cooker." This was a tin-topped chest I often used as a bench in Gamma's kitchen. Three deep wells held the metal pots with their twist-on lids. I think it may have been electric, but its prototype was obvious. Like the Bean Hole Bean Supper here in Cushing, it took 24 hours to do the job. Tasty? Oh my! When we went to a potluck supper, all the ladies said, "You and your grandma make the best beans!" It must have been true, because her huge brown crock always came home empty.

Monday was Wash Day and I was a real help there too. Only the bottom sheets were stripped from the beds (It's the soiled one, Deah, because you lie on it") and tossed halfway down the steep stairs. Then I prodded and kicked until they heaped at ground level.

Back then there were no fitted sheets. The top one merely became the bottom. I struggled to make hospital corners like Gramma's, and soon gained the strength to lift and tuck until they held tight pretty much all week.

A Gampa-made stool boosted me to washing machine height. This shiny copper monster with long legs growled ominously and marched across the linoleum floor during the wash cycle. The two of us together had to push it back against the wall ("One, two three – *heave!*")

After that, Gammy dragged out the water-sodden sheets and towels and started them through the wringer while I pushed the button. Hers was the harder job, but mine was safer and more fun. "I start one corner first, Deah. If it bunches up it won't fit through. Now turn it on."

We hauled the flattened mass in a great laundry basket out to the back yard, (when Gampa added wheels it was much easier to manage) and secured everything, from linens to socks, with clothespins. Gammy tugged and smoothed each sheet so it wouldn't have to be ironed the next day. She hated ironing sheets. "I know someone who irons her socks! Can you imagine that?" Gammy loved laughing.

I was much too old to take a nap but, after one of Gamma's workday projects, a soft pillow ("Pull the spread down first, Deah.") in the August heat was more than welcome.

Was it all drudgery? Hardly! My grandmother was practical. "If you haven't finished your chores by nine in the morning, you haven't planned your day at all well," she said with a wink.

And Gamma was a gardener. Her little heaven glowed with triumphant, towering hollyhocks and blue and yellow flag iris. She said that her orange trumpet vines called the hummingbirds all the way from South America. (We tried to toot a flower, but no sound came out.)

Gampa worked along side her to make this tiny spot a paradise. In the far corner he constructed a craggy rock garden and an oval pool that Gammy filled with water lilies – flat green pads and huge blossoms. On the hillside behind the pool, little pansy-faced Johnny Jump-Ups pranced among green Hens-and-Chickens. No wonder that my parents wedding party was held in this enchanted garden.

When Gampa turned the spigot on ever so slowly, the three of us sprawled on the warm grass to watch the show. Water rose silently in a deep-shadowed grotto, spilled over the lip, filled the next canal, then slid down a stairway of stones to spill again.

We gasped when the stream found the last smooth rock and plunged eighteen inches to the fishpond below. From our grass-level view it was our own Niagra. We cheered and clapped and grinned. Surprise! From under the lily pads, up from the black depths, rose the first of several sea-monsters – a foot-long orange whale with mouth wide open, loudly sucking fresh water. Oh, it was a glorious finale!

Who fed these monster goldfish? Each sunny morning, I picked Japanese beetles and rose bugs off the flowers (tickling my palms) and brushed them wriggling into the pool before they could fly away. A flash of fish and the dreadful deed was done!

Gampa had built a long garden bench, its trellis supporting a thick canopy of red roses. "Can you smell the perfume, Deah? Sit heah." Oh yes – sweet smell from above along with the hum of bees. Leaning against Gamma's arm, looking up, I saw sunlight blushing through the petals, and a lazy butterfly.

Each time I sat on that bench, I knew a pure, safe and flawless world. Today, sixty years later, I can still feel the scratch of cracking paint on the backs of my thin bare legs.

&

I have several purposes for telling you these mundane things in such detail: first, to honor this woman who meant little to the world, but everything to me. I believe she ought to be remembered, and these vignettes may give the reader some sense of her person, her strong character and timeless values. She kept in touch with many people, writing several letters each day. Her last notes were penned less than a week before her death at ninety four. "I take each day as it comes, my Deah" was no idle comment.

Secondly, this small record of a distant time and a great-great grandmother they could never meet is a small gift for my own grandchildren.

Last but not least, I hope you've been carried back for a moment to your own place of childish innocence, because I'm setting the stage to share with you a gift from my grandmother's garden.

A FAIRY'S TRAVEL CASE

Folklore is ephemeral. What may seem solid truth to one generation may disappear entirely in the very next. I've talked with thirty women of my age or older, and not one knew the secret hidden in the blossom of a bleeding heart. In fact, I phoned "Cousin Barbara" as I was writing this story, and even she, my grandmother's own niece, now eighty-eight, had never heard of it.

One summer afternoon, Gammy and I were seated on the garden bench. "I want to show you something very wonderful," she explained, holding in her open hand a single bleeding heart flower.

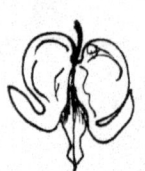 "It's perfect," I said, staring at the plump pink-red heart. It seemed indeed to be bleeding – red petals twisted way back to reveal a white inside dripping out through the bottom – a mature flower, just right for her demonstration.)

"Ehyuh, and it has a secret too. It's really a fairy suitcase." (Instantly I imagined a fairy sitting on her thumb.) "A fairy needs a pair of animals to pull her carriage," Gamma

90

continued. Grasping the heart close to the stem at the very outer edges, she pulled it gently apart and set the two petals on their hollow bottoms.

"What do you see?"

I didn't have to guess. "Bunnies!" I exclaimed. "Pink bunnies!"

Gamma merely smiled. "Imagine *your* carriage drawn by two fuschia-pink rabbits."

"And if she's going to a party, she'll need jewelry," Gamma went on, pulling apart the next layer.

I was astonished and delighted when she laid. on the garden seat. a perfect pair of delicate earrings with hanging gold drops.

"Should she have dancing slippers?"

I nodded, speechless. *Slippers?* That would be impossible even for my magical grandmother to conjure up!

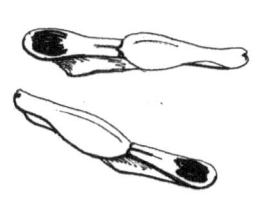

But a pair of strapless 'glass slippers' trembled slightly in the summer breeze, dark wear-marks inside the heels, just exactly like my own shoes! And the bottom was almost a runner, not a heel. For skating on the water of the fishpond on a moonlit summer night, do you suppose?

"One last thing," Gammy whispered, her fist closed and held tantalizingly toward me. "What does every fairy carry?"

I thought and thought. "Is it a magic wand?"

Gammy slowly opened her fingers and there it was – a long wand with a gold star on top!

And now, nothing was left of the original flower but the tiniest stem.

~

The contents of this fairy case lay on my bedside table all night. Oh, I wanted to keep them forever, but in the morning they'd shriveled to almost nothing. That's the way with fairy things.

&

Will you share this little surprise with the girls you know – daughters and granddaughters, and maybe neighbor children too? (Not forgetting the ones whose hair has become gray. We still remember fairies.)

But wait. I believe this is more than a "girl thing," so don't leave out the boys. We all need wonder in our lives and perhaps Grandfathers can lead the way here.

I must admit that my very own daughter didn't learn of this little fantasy until she was already a mother herself, and I was sharing the story with my granddaughter. The truth is that you need the flower itself to jog the memory. Happily, where I live now a grand bleeding heart is reborn beside my front door every spring.

To carry this idea even further, plant a bleeding heart if you haven't one already, or bring one to the garden of a friend. Then you, too, will be able to pass on this fanciful fact and – one open heart at a time – knowledge of this whimsical gift will multiply.

I wonder how far it will travel, don't you?

HOLIDAY
LIGHTS

HOLIDAY LIGHTS

I am aghast. This year, by the first of November, stores were already dragging out their tinsel finery, bludgeoning our senses with neon-phony Holiday glitz. Newscasts announced it with hardly a murmur of outrage. Last year I muttered peevishly that pre-Thanksgiving decorations would soon be flung in our faces – praying all the while that I was wrong. Indeed my predictions proved horribly true – Halloween orange-and-black followed a mere 24 hours later by Christmas red-and-green!

Where is that innocent holiday spirit we call forth each season from the depth of our child-selves? It seems to be buried far beneath greed and gimmee. Do the merchants understand it may all backfire one day? Well, we can protest to the owners of the stores we patronize, if it seems important enough, but I take to heart an important message. Do you recall it? After the Grinch stole all the Christmas "stuff," Dr. Seuss reminded us that, "Christmas came just the same."

It's like the lights on our homes. They're not a sales gimmick, but a family's wish to share the joy of the holidays. I remember well from my childhood an elderly couple's astonishing gift to our town. They looped thousands of lights on their fences and trees and eaves, then added dozens of deerstatues&santas&sleighs&angels&sixfootcandles, oh my!

Admittedly it went a dite overboard, but many, many people made annual pilgrimages to view the display. Traffic backed up. Neighbors took to complaining. But I drove slowly by in the piercing cold one December evening, peering into the windows of passing cars. I assure you that the looks of wonder on children's faces – open mouthed breaths steaming glass – said it all.

When I was young, my father and I played "opposites." What is the opposite of High? Low. And of Yes? No. But then he tricked me: Love? No, not Hate, but Indifference. And the hardest one to grasp: that Dark is not the opposite of Light, but merely the absence of light. When we went to church on Christmas Eve – an enormous stone edifice with vaulted ceilings and deep shadows – a single candle on the altar was ceremonially set alight. In a flash the darkness vanished. My father explained that a thousand tons of dark never snuffs out even one tiny flame.

✳✳✳

Last year I was again reminded of the symbolic power of Lights.

But first, since you may never visit Cushing, Maine, let me set the stage for you. My tiny village, bordered by the St. George and Meduncook Rivers, sprawls across a granite-and-green peninsula stretching more than ten miles toward the cold, deep waters of the Atlantic Ocean. River Road begins at the Thomaston Bridge that spans the St. George, then lazily meanders toward the Gut, passing old capes and trailers, farmhouses and ponds, sheep and horses, meadows and fields, evergreen woods and distant glimpses of river and bay – all comfortably spaced out with room enough to breathe. Dirt fire-roads lead to year 'round homes and summer cottages nestled in the woods or gracing the edge of the St. George. Some dwellings nearer the Point face on deep water and are unquestionably elegant.

Fales General Store, about 6 miles from the Thomaston Bridge, is a focal point of Cushing; its most meaningful staples are community concerns and simple small town friendliness. The owners, in a very real sense I believe, both set *and* reflect the tone of the town.

If you keep going straight at the store you soon come upon our Firehouse and brand-new Community School. (The old school is about to become our Town Hall. We are growing, and some think of it as Progress.). The long road to the Gut changes its name from River Road to Pleasant Point as it turns just after Fales. Soon you pass our community church – a simple building with a short, square steeple, deep green shutters and that indescribable aura of resolute Maine spirit. A mile or so further you come upon the Acorn Grange Hall that has welcomed its members for a hundred years or so. Hathorne Road, off to the left, eventually reaches the Olson House, where Andrew Wyeth painted so many magnificent scenes evocative of stolid Maine spirit. Then comes the Post Office. The next right is Salt Pond Road, which leads to the larger neighboring town of Friendship.

It takes another few miles for Pleasant Point Road to dwindle into a delta of paths and the last homes on the Point. Here are a gathering of sailboats and lobster boats and good salt water. At the Gut, people can cross the flats to Gay Island when the "mudzin" at low tide. Finally, a sign proclaims "TOWNSEND." (And so it is, but the truth is that the Townsends live there.) Along this whole stretch of country road from the bridge to the gut no cement sidewalks or streetlights impinge on our tranquility.

I often say that I never need to cross the green Thomaston Bridge, because everything one needs is here in the town of Cushing. Of course I didn't know that when I was younger, and believed that it was necessary to go to "The City" for entertainment.

Let's go back now and turn onto Salt Pond Road. Imagine a cold winter night near Christmas. Breath forms in great clouds before your face and a full moon makes the squeaky snow sparkle. A double-treat awaits us in the dark: the moonlit evening soon gives way to the glow of floodlights high on a sparse hill. The Old South Cushing Baptist Church, lately acquired by the Historical Society, stands bathed in light, wreathes hung on its doors made huge by deep-shadowed electric brilliance.

No longer used for weekly services, it is still a symbol of enduring community values. Several activities take place there during the summer and, before closing up for the winter, we gather for a program of Harvest Songs. "All the sheaves are gathered in ere the winter storms begin."

Picture the solitude. On this winding side road, on this small peninsula, far from any appreciable population to enjoy the sight, stands this glowing church – more visible from the ocean than from Pleasant Point Road. Coming upon it is always a glorious surprise.

And it is truly a gift of light. Every year, Doug and Brenda Adams, the church's next-door neighbors, floodlight the building as their unique gift to all of Cushing. Neighbors indeed, but not so very close! Doug must first of all drag several hundred feet of orange electric cord through the woods.

Now this dark, winding country road holds another gift of lights. Just last year the Kinne and Haynes families (the next house after the Adams, yet a full half-mile further on) gave a special Christmas present to grandfather Alan Kinne, who was gravely ill. Afterwards, Alan sent an email to the people of the Town of Cushing.

Oh yes, I wanted you to know that this little town has a community email system set up by Chet Knowles. We call him our Town Crier. Every few days he sends us all a message – the email address of a new resident, perhaps, or a plea for news of a lost pet, or an invitation to a potluck supper to benefit someone in need. It all adds to the sense of community.

Rather than describe the circumstances to you, here's are Alan's own words – his email to Cushing:

A Christmas Story 2002

With all the bad news and frightening things going on, it is so wonderful to be able, at this time of year, to tell a story of kindness and giving.

On this past Sunday (December 8, 2002) we had a visit from our grand daughter Abby Haynes (9) and her friend Aurora Aiken (7). The story we got was, they were bored and wanted to play over at Gram and Pupa's house. They had written a list of things to do and games to play. I thought it a little strange, however it sounded like fun. Next thing I knew they had set up their activities in the guest room and our 'office', and those two rooms be- came off limits for June and myself. It happens that those two rooms overlook our driveway. June had gone off to church and I became a little inquisitive, like why couldn't I go into the office, what's going on, how long are you

staying here etc. I received very vague answers and "it's a surprise".

The day progressed and they got my lunch and cleaned up the kitchen all the time with cute smiles on their faces and "unknowing" looks. June came home and got the same story about where she could go in the house and where she couldn't. We asked how long they were staying and the response was "'til about 4:30".

Along about 2:30, Juli arrived and said "Get your portable oxygen, Dad, and both of you put your coats on and come with me." She had the car started and warm. We went out to the car and rode halfway up our driveway and
Lo and Behold . . .

At the end of our driveway is a beautiful tree about 40 feet tall and all around it stood children and adults watching and helping Scott Strong from Central Maine Power work his magic with his "cherry picker", string lights on this gorgeous tree. (Not only did he donate his time and CMP truck on this day but also gave up most of his football game). Assisting him was the Leader and six Boy Scouts from Troop #214 out of Thomaston.

While we sat and watched the finishing touches, we all had hot chocolate and home made cookies, made by Ashley Aiken and our granddaughter Kaitlyn Haynes. Friends and family had been invited to partake of the goodies, share in the joy and friendship and watch the lighting of the tree.

Needless to say we were overwhelmed by the gift of the lights (4500 of them!) from our children Juli and Scott and their families, and most importantly the gift of time and effort by all those who made this possible.

What a wonderful day and what wonderful nights we will have, sitting together looking at this beautiful expression of the Christmas Season.

Happy Holidays, and Peace, to one and all.

June and Alan Kinne

***

Beautiful and touching indeed!

Alan will not be enjoying the lights with his family this year, but his memory lives on in many wonderful ways, and one that is sure to gleam for all of us again and for many years to come is his Christmas tree on Salt Pond Road.

Juli promises.

If you are unable to visit Cushing, then simply close your eyes and imagine a leisurely trip down our peninsula at dusk. The houses thin out to piney woods, the road darkens, a turn onto Salt Pond Road and you are face to face with a glowing place of worship and soon after with a towering tree of lights. They are visions to remember, especially when you know the stories behind their creation.

* * *

May every illumination you come upon this holiday remind you of the love and joy of the Season.

XXX

WONDER!

*W*ONDER!

Webster's Dictionary says:

Won"der\, n.
    That emotion which is excited by novelty, or the presentation to the sight or mind of something new, unusual, strange, great, extraordinary, or not well understood; surprise; astonishment; admiration; amazement.

♪   ♪   ♪

    My parents instilled a sense of wonder in me. When I was small, every day was an adventure, and thankfully that attitude remains true even now. From them, I learned that wonder – that quick joyful intake of breath (inspiration?) – is at the center of life.

    They read to me – always with the pleasure of cuddling up together and the thrill of something fascinating or spectacular leaping from the page.

    Or we lay on the grass to observe an ant colony's long line of march, each tiny creature carrying creamy white seeds my parents assured me were their babies all wrapped up in swaddling clothes.

    We stood chilled in our backyard in the autumn darkness, astonished by streaks of glowing green and pink as Northern Lights rippled across the sky, and discovered Orion's belt and sword in the twinkling stars.

* * *

Only a couple of years ago, my grandson Andrew was visiting me here in Cushing. The summer evening was warm, but the stars were sharp and clear, the Milky Way a bright glowing path that swept across the sky directly over the house.

"Look, Andrew. Do you see that wide band of white clouds across the sky?" "Uh, huh," he said, a little bored. "That's the Milky Way," I continued. "Not clouds at all, but billions of far, far away suns, billions of stars ..."

We were quiet.

Suddenly he stood up straight, swung his head rapidly from horizon to horizon. "Ohhh...," Deep intake of breath, perception shifting as wonder floods the soul – (You know that feeling) –

His voice was a throaty whisper: "Oh, Gramma ... billions ... and ... billions ... of ... STARS!"

* * *

Wonder because of the stars is no greater really than a child's wonder at the glow of a Christmas tree's lights. I still squint to see the angel lights saturating my vision, just as my mother taught me to do 65 or more years ago. Way back then, the light bulbs were big and fat, remember? – not at all like today's sparkling little wheat-lights.

The Christmas Season is full of wonder and promise, reminding me of our Creator's love and His myriad gifts to us. It is, however, laced with a certain poignancy, for we as a people have not yet shown our earth and all its creatures the respect and love they deserve. Our stewardship is a deep responsibility. I pray some day we'll get it right.

Have you ever thought that the computer acts as a twenty-first Century guru whose ideas race around the world? Of course much of it is nonsense: silly sayings, tasteless cartoons and divisive opinions. But good messages light my PC screen too. They come to me from friends across the country, multiplying like dandelions, so fast I may delete them instead of paying close attention, even when the message is profound – like this email I received recently. Let me share it with you. On the subject line was written:

"Seven Wonders of the World."

A group of students were asked to list what they thought were the present "Seven Wonders of the World." Though there were some disagreements, the following received the most votes:

1. Egypt's Great Pyramids
2. The Taj Mahal
3. The Grand Canyon
4. The Panama Canal
5. The Empire State Building
6. St. Peter's Basilica
7. China's Great Wall

While gathering the votes, the teacher noted that one student had not finished her paper yet. So she asked the girl if she was having trouble with her list. The girl replied,

"Yes, a little. I couldn't quite make up my mind because there were so many."

The teacher said, "Well, tell us what you have, and maybe we can help."

The girl hesitated, then read, "I think the 'Seven Wonders of the World' are:

1. To See
2. To Hear
3. To Touch
4. To Taste
5. To Feel
6. To Laugh, and
7. To Love."

The room was so quiet you could have heard a pin drop.

The things we overlook -- so simple and ordinary that we take them for granted -- are truly wondrous!

This is a gentle reminder – that the most precious things in life cannot be built by hand or bought by man.

And the email finished, as so many of them do, with a cheerful admonishment:

"Don't be too busy to pass this message on."

* * *

Every year I write a Christmas message to you, my dear friends and acquaintances, who have touched my life in some way. You may call what's in my heart trite -- that is, commonplace and unoriginal -- but I know that the trite is also true.

Here are my personal wishes for all of us, that we . . .

Don't become too busy -- during the holidays and all year through.

Allow the wonder of this gift of life to fill our hearts.

Find the spirit of the Season lasting far beyond New Year's Day.

Discover Joy, and share it with everyone.

Find that deep sense of inner peace spreading from each one of us to the next.

Believe with certainty that it is possible to bring peace to every heart alive in this wonder-filled home we call Earth.

* * *

LUNCH
WITH LUTHERA

*L*UNCH
WITH *L*UTHERA

Every year by early October, a small corner of my brain shifts into holiday alert, casting about casually for this year's message to you. And every year it reveals itself unexpectedly, as I learn (again!) to practice patience. Driving along Cushing's country roads, filling my eyes with the glorious colors of fall, the ritual of Recalling Christmas Past comes naturally.

Old(er) age, and the season, release surprising memories. This one popped from the ancient vaults of my gray matter, perhaps more vividly real now than it was fifty-five years ago:

My mother and father liked gifts that lasted beyond the holidays, calling them "permanent presents" or "on-going gifts." One year it was two tickets for a series of six matinees at Carnegie Hall. I had written permission to leave high school at noon every other Friday. Imagine it! Legal hooky in a Christmas present! Sometimes one of my parents and I climbed aboard the Lackawanna train; at other times it was a school friend. Right now in detail I can recall soaring music, an applauding audience, and the thrumming energy of the City. Permanent? Oh yes -- a gift for a lifetime! I was just fifteen.

* * *

Luthera Dawson and I met soon after I read "Saltwater Farm," her charming book about her childhood in Cushing. She is 24 years older than I, and one day we were talking about the importance of friends. Being "from away," I was in need of new ones. Luthera admitted that her advancing years meant that close friends were leaving her life, so she too needed new contacts. We solved this problem with Lunch – with a capital "L."

This gift, given and received during my first year in Cushing, wasn't exchanged during the holidays, but, right from the beginning, we knew this simple idea possessed _everything._ It was wrapped in the joy of giving, designed to renew monthly, expandable to fit every size, and filled both of us with anticipation and high spirits.

A couple of friends were invited, and we met at our favorite seafood restaurant. We loved it. But Luthera vehemently did not. Her Cushing childhood, filled with a plethora of coastal cooking, had not endeared her to fruits-of-the-sea. But _lunching_ with Luthera took off instantly -- a gathering of mostly graying (or is that whitening?) women expecting to laugh with strangers and old friends. What else to name it but "Off Our Rockers."

It all began in nineteen ninety-seven. If you want Rockers statistics, I'll give just a few. In these 9 years, several dozen women have joined with us. The age-spread is 35 to 94; the furthest from home were born in Montana and England. Every one of the original gang is still faithful to the group. We have dined grandly at restaurants near and far (with but a few less-than-perfect dishes and experiences.) The prices of gas and lunch have risen surprisingly fast! The weather often prevents January and February meetings, but the laziest days of summer find us next to the rocky coast, enthralled by the view as we enjoy a burger or a lobster roll, looking like tourists at our picnic table amid cries of laughter from the circling seagulls.

One day, a dozen of us gathered at a single long table at the Sail Loft in Rockport. (Fine food, good harbor view.) I don't know how it started, but we were soon telling off-color stories and reacting with staccato bursts of loud laughter. A distinguished looking gentleman stopped on his way to pay his tab. "That," he said with a genuine smile, "is the most wonderful, raucous laughter." I glanced over at Luthera. Seated by the window, where she could not easily get away, she seemed to have slid rather far down in her chair. Was it the result of helpless laughter or, more likely, to indicate we were all total strangers to her and she was merely there for the view?

The Sail Loft closed very soon after. We think we were not really the cause.

Sometimes interest in Lunch has ebbed – "we're all so busy," someone may say – and then Luthera will phone: "Isn't Rockers next week?" And I'll hurry to make some calls and contact the restaurant we chose the month before. Reserving a table, it's fun to tell the Manager, "The group is Off Our Rockers."

Certainly It's not unusual for a group of women to have lunch together once a month, but this gang is special because it is our group -- a bit like the Red Hat Society but simpler, with a plain Maine touch. And of interest to me is the fact that half of us are "from away, here to stay" while the other half are native Mainers. So in a real way our original mission has continued, as we gather for the pleasure of each other's company.

Now, at age 70, I'm ever more aware of the fading importance of material things. What did the Grinch discover after he had stolen all the Who's gifts? That Christmas…

> "…came without ribbons! It came without tags!
> It came without packages, boxes or bags!"

I thank each of you Rockers for being part of my life. You may come with ribbons, but surely not with tags! Each time, I eagerly look forward to Lunch with you because a Rockers Lunch is *always* fun.

And thank you, Luthera, for this remarkably renewable, on-going gift.

I am still laughing because, as I sat typing the previous page, Luthera called to say, "Is Rockers meeting this month? I want to put something more fun than a doctor's appointment to on my Calendar."

* * *

$\mathscr{T}$he message to you for this year is simple and self-evident. Of course I wish you the material things you may truly need – safety and food, security and warmth -- especially in this year of soaring fuel prices.

Most of all I wish you renewable gifts this holiday season – that is, spiritual memories and happy activities for every day and to last your whole year through -- gifts wrapped in joy, affection, humor and camaraderie.

If we could, wouldn't we want this to be our unending gift to the whole world?

A
FLOCK OF HOPE

By
Judith M. Knowlton

$\mathscr{A}$ $\mathscr{F}$LOCK OF $\mathscr{H}$OPE

Perceiving all of Life as gifts isn't a new concept to me. As a small child, I was taught by my family that gifts come in a myriad forms, and most of them are not wrapped in tissue and tinsel.

The purist gifts are given freely, with no strings attached. The value? Certainly not measured in size or money – like a plate of muffins to welcome a new neighbor, the offer of a helping hand, or an invitation to picnic on the rocky Maine coast.

Every day presents me with the most delight-ful gifts just beyond my computer. The window faces west, where a high hedge separates the property from River Road. Every spring, once I fill the feeder with thistle seed and the hedge thickens with budding leaves, the view is magical. Dozens of vibrant, burnished-yellow blossoms nestle motionless among the branches or sway in the breeze -- then suddenly flash off to the feeder. Goldfinches by the dozens! Believe me, I remember to say thank you!

That same window mesmerizes me with the endless passage of sunsets above the dark pointed pines on the hill. They may be pinkish pale, gold and fuchsia; crimson streaked with scarlet, or pewter gray before the snow -- every one an inspiring, ephemeral gift.

It must be true that every gift begins as a thought –
since all that ever was, is now or ever will be is present in
the mind of God.

We human beings have inflicted our world with
another hard year of anger and war, despite the rising
awareness of global warming and the need to act with
intelligence -- and quickly. Every issue has been entwined
with the perennial braying of politicians. They may be truly
concerned, but human government is unwieldy at best. I
often feel helpless to make a difference, but want so much to
be part of the solution!

Several years ago I discovered something I could whole-
heartedly take part in: "The Four-Footed Attack Against
Hunger." The rest of this Christmas message comes almost
entirely from "The Most Important Gift Catalog in the World,"
Heifer International. You'll find it at www.catalog.heifer.org

Here's the story:

A Midwestern farmer named Dan West was ladling
out rations of milk to hungry children during the Spanish Civil
War when it hit him. *"These children don't need a cup, they
need a cow."*
West, serving as a Church of the Brethren relief
worker, was forced to decide who would receive the limited
rations and who wouldn't – literally, who would live, and who
would die. This kind of aid, he knew, would never be
enough.
When West returned home in 1938, he worked to
form Heifers for Relief, dedicated to ending hunger
permanently by providing families with *livestock and training*

so that they "could be spared the indignity of depending on others to feed their children."

By 1944, the first shipment of 17 heifers left York, Pennsylvania, for Puerto Rico, going to families whose malnourished children had never even tasted milk. Why heifers? Because these young cows haven't yet given birth, they are perfect for supplying a continued source of milk. They are a continued source of support, because each family agrees to "pass on the gift" by donating the female offspring to another family. The gift of food is never-ending.

This simple idea of giving families a source of food rather than short-term relief caught on and has continued for close to 60 years. As a result, millions of families in 115 countries are experiencing better health, more income and the joy of helping others. Why not browse through their website?   www.heifer.org

If you are not computer savvy, make a phone call: (800) 422-0474. Ask them for a paper catalog filled with pictures and individual stories. It is sure to warm your heart and stimulate your imagination.

Close your eyes for just a moment. Envision yourself living in a third-world country with little food, few prospects, hardscrabble living. The children are often hungry. Not at all like your own life, is it? Now imagine that a flock of geese arrives in your dooryard, along with training to assure their good health. The huge eggs are delicious; the children are thrilled. How quickly their small bodies and outlook improve! Watch the fuzzy gray goslings hatch and grow. Soon you can share the birds with your neighbors, and your village is transformed . . .

All this can be accomplished with one original $60 contribution – yours!

Heifer's "Flock of Hope" is my own yearly donation, because it consists of chicks, ducks and/or goslings, depending on the climate and needs of the culture. I used to raise ducks and geese and now imagine my new "flock of hope" expanding every year.

FOOD, TRACTOR and TRUCK!

Do you have difficulty imagining the importance of a single animal to a family? For many, the Water Buffalo is a literal lifesaver. Here's what Heifer's catalog says:

"A single water buffalo can lead a hungry family out of poverty and give them a chance for a bright future filled with hope and free from hunger. Water buffalo provide draft power for planting rice and potatoes, milk for protein and manure for fertilizer and fuel.

"In fact, a farmer can plant FOUR TIMES more rice with a buffalo than by hand! And a water buffalo can haul loads to market – where the sale of extra produce brings in vital income for clothing, medicine and school.

"Plus, by renting their buffalo to neighbors, Heifer families can earn even more money for home improvements or a variety of livestock."

"If I die, my family will weep for me.
If my buffalo dies, my family will starve."
Thai farmer

The Heifer gift of a water buffalo is $250.
A "share" is only $25.

Or .... choose the spectacular! – *for* $5,000, a group can buy together:

A WHOLE ARK

Changing the World Two by Two

2 cows, to bring milk and income to a Russian village.

2 sheep, to help families in New Mexico produce wool.

2 camels, to help families in Kenya earn income by transporting agricultural and industrial materials.

2 oxen, to pull plows and carts in Uganda.

2 water buffalo, to help Indonesian families increase rice production through animal draft power.

2 pigs, to enable families in Cambodia to attain greater self-reliance.

2 beehives, to help families in Kentucky earn money through the sale of honey and beeswax.

2 goats, to help Guatemalan families provide milk for their families and earn extra income.

2 donkeys, to supply animal draft power for famers in Tanzania.

2 trios of ducks to help families in Ghana generate income through the sale of eggs and birds.

2 trios of rabbits to provide food and income for families in North Korea.

2 trios of guinea pigs to help families in Peru add protein to their diets and increase income.

2 flocks of chicks to help families in South Africa improve nutrition and generate income through the sale of eggs.

2 llamas to improve livestock bloodlines and produce wool and income for Bolivian families.

2 flocks of geese to help families in China better their nutrition and income through the production of eggs and meat.

The price of a gift ark includes the purchase/transport of high quality animals and the training/support that Heifer International gives recipients. Contributions to the Gift Ark program represent a contribution to the entire mission of Heifer. Donations will be used where they are needed most. Heifer International is a non-profit 501 (c)(3) organization.

This season, and for the coming years, may the love your gifts symbolize expand in ways we hardly dare imagine, until they embrace our whole earth.

XXX

FLYING HIGH

FLYING HIGH

Autumn is already upon us as I write.

A splash of orange leaves signals the change, and an awe-inspiring full orange moon, but it's unseasonably warm for a Maine Fall, and glorious blue skies are swiftly erased by heavy fog.

Nevertheless, it's time for me to think about my Christmas card. Perhaps you know how satisfying it is for me to plan one: from the first idea, to writing, to designing, to printing, to addressing, then at last sending it afar to new acquaintances, and dear old friends. It's a spiritual journey -- my gift to you, and most certainly to myself, at the same time.

These little booklets have made me more consciously grateful for my blessings, piled high as they are, gift upon gift, joy upon joy, not wrapped in bright paper and tied with tinsel, but woven into the fabric of my experience.

Bald eagle, blue heron, fox, coyote, and moose are seen regularly on Cushing's peninsula. It is a rural community of narrow roads, no streetlights, and glimpses of the St. George River and Broad Cove. The open ocean is visible in several places, from private property, and old apple trees grow close to the road, dropping unpicked fruit along the shoulder, where they spread out in patches of yellow or red be-neath their trees. Meadows and woods separate the homes, and expansive hay fields are still common.

The emotional center of town is Fales General Store. It's just exactly what you would hope for: gas and oil, friendly talk, all the staples, and some surprising new additions, like a pesto that Kelly, the youngest Fales, makes fresh. (It is superb on absolutely everything, except probably ice cream. In any case, I am addicted!)

A hayfield of several acres, across the road, is aptly named "The Pancake." Level and nearly round, except where the road has cut off a piece, Richard Fales regularly mows a path along the whole edge of it for the walkers, and has placed two Adirondack chairs at the half-way-around point. Beyond them, pebbly beach and partly submersed rocks define the edge of Broad Cove – no crash of surf or open ocean, but sparkling salt water, sand pipers, and the wet shine of the flats when "mudzin," or "tidezout." Both the Pancake and Fales are quintessential Cushing to me.

I believe that every single thing in this wondrous world begins with an idea, from baking a cake to butterflies to Broad Cove. The Kite Flight came about in the same way; the thought of it had been percolating slowly over time in my mind.

Here's how it happened:

Often, driving by slowly and looking out across the field at the Cove, I've glimpsed a flurry of kites, but it was only my imagination at work. Wouldn't a kite day be fun? When I mentioned it to several people, there was only mild interest. Nevertheless, more than a year ago, I asked Elaine Fales if we could have a kite-flying day on the Pancake. Oh yes, she thought it would be fun too, but only after the mowing, and please not to drive on the field.

More time passed, but I hadn't forgotten. Several of us were enjoying our weekly Saturday morning breakfast at Broad Cove Church. (It's the most delicious menu, with a fine fresh fruit cup, and a must-do activity in summer) when I mentioned flying kites on the Pancake, and Neville Lewis responded instantly. "Sounds great. What do we have to do?"

And *that* is how an idea blossoms into reality.

I stopped at the store on the way home. The Fales family was instantly enthusiastic. John promised to get official approval as soon as possible from his parents, Elaine and Richard -- and here, once again, I thank them for their gracious approval.

We quickly agreed upon a date -- the Saturday of Labor Day weekend, September the First -- because it seemed a fitting farewell to summer, and a happy send-off for our summer guests. September Second was proclaimed the rain or no-wind date, but we knew that this Cushing Kite Flight might be pushed into October, if all the variables failed to mesh perfectly.

The day could not be rainy, and the wind must be just right – not too strong and blustery, and certainly not dead calm! We were told that spring is best for kites. "But, why not now?" we

133

responded. Remember, we could use the hayfield only *after* it had been mowed.

Time of day was critical too. Russ Penney said to check the tide chart first, because incoming tides usually mean a stronger wind. Out came a chart. High tide that afternoon would be 2:39, so 11 AM to 3 PM seemed perfect. Four full hours of flying. Excitement was mounting!

Organizing was part of the pleasure. Posters pro-claimed *"Bring your own kite and folding chair!"* Chet Knowles, who e-mails community announcements to the whole Town, asked who was sponsoring the event. "Spontaneous, not sponsored," I emailed back. Neville offered to bring a large table, the Ambulance Squad agreed to sell bottled water, and Kelly promised to serve hotdogs at the store. Merely mention a need and someone said, "I'll do it!"

The project was taking shape nicely!

Then I found Bob Ray on the internet. He used to own a kite place in Portland, and was instantly enthusiastic, offering to provide us with extra lines and reel handles, but his main service was suggesting a simple kite kit. It consisted of an ordinary white paper bag, with a smiley face in marker pen (or any other do-it-yourself picture), two sticks, a line and reel, a string bridle, and two tails made from colorful surveyor's tape. Bob guaranteed satisfaction. We decided that every child, young or old, deserved the gift of a kite; we would leave no one out!

I thought the bag kites looked more like bumble bees – not quite aerodynamically sound! -- but we trusted that Bob knew his business. Russ took them home, thinking to make one ahead of time for practice, but ended up making several.

Just like Christmas, we older children waited with anticipation so real we could taste it. "Are you flying a kite?" we asked everyone we met. The answers were exuberant, matching the sparkle in their eyes. Some bought new rigs, but many were hauling out vintage kites that had been languishing in attics. You can be sure they carried fond memories of faraway times and places.

But first we had to wait for the mowing!

What a welcome sight! A swarm of haymaking equipment – tractors, cutters, balers, and huge hay baskets -- arrived on the Pancake with 2 weeks to spare, but then it showered or rained almost every other day, quite enough to make mowing impossible.

I learned that haymaking is an art made up of weather, mature plants, and the farmer's experienced sense of "readiness." Cut it too soon or too wet, and spontaneous combustion can result in a surprise fire and a lost barn. Oddly enough, wet hay, with moisture of more than 22%, is more likely to combust than dry hay. (Research on the internet is so easy!)

We checked the weatherman's predictions constantly, hoping that September First would be sunny, with a decent, steady wind. Yes, that was important. But we also needed a three-day string of sunny days to transform the field from high hay to pancake plane. Only one date was feasible. What if the farmer was too busy to take advantage?

Then one morning Russ stopped by on his way to work with a grin on his face. Haying had begun -- and none too soon either. It was only about a week to September.

* * *

Kite-day dawned sunny, breezy and cool. I slid my 30 year old, six-sided box kite into the back of the car with 4 molded plastic chairs, and headed for the Pancake. We had agreed to meet by 10:30, but as I pulled over the hill a full hour early, I saw that several people had gathered, and one kite was already airborne!

And they came: little children with wondering eyes, the young, the younger at heart like me, carrying an astonishing variety of kites. A row of assorted chairs quickly expanded along the bank next to the road, backed by a longer line of cars. People passed to and fro from Fales; hotdogs with mustard began to sell early in the day.

The flyers, many I didn't know, spread out across the meadow, giving each other plenty of room. Ann Guild brought an exotic dragon. Roley James assisted anyone who required that second set of hands for take-off. John Flint, omni-present pipe clenched in his teeth, brought a complicated contraption that never flew. Once assembled, he decided to hang it in his attic rather than attempt solving *that* puzzle again! Bob Ellis's parafoil swooped and soared in the far distance. A huge multi-colored delta, with a myriad ribbons, rose effortlessly and hung in the sky for a very long time. Several men carted their lawn chairs to satisfactory locations, and then sat placidly in the center of their kingdoms, their kites hovering serenely far above their heads. Trish Weisbrot's blue tadpole danced in the wind. Crystal and Chris Robinson's two-line stunt kite swept into the air, and then dove sharply into the ground. "Needs tail, more tail!" shouted the experts in the front row. "More tail" became the day's mantra. The tailgate of Russ's truck held everything. Sure enough, with several more yards of tail, the rebellious kite came under complete control. We were entranced by Crystal's performance – a ballet of skill and grace. Applause rippled across the meadow!

My own kite rose easily, but failed to maintain height because of too-light winds close to the ground – until John Duffy arrived with his extraordinary line and reel. He had brought a *fishing pole!* Just imagine it: so easy to let out and reel in! Attaching the line to my kite, he allowed it to race for the clouds so fast that his thumb was burned as he tried to brake. At last my old kite reached the stupendous height it was made for! I was truly satisfied.

The paper-bag kites were nothing less than phenomenal! Russ, acting as teacher and guide, placed a kite in the hands of any child who wanted one. How do you describe rapture and total concentration in a small one's face? They were well and truly mesmerized, as their small kites rose effortlessly and stayed aloft.

Then there was one teenage boy. He was too old to get involved in such nonsense – simply too bored, too disengaged. And yet ... when Russ handed his kite to him, it leapt high in the air instantly. The young man became, you know, *interested!* Soon after, we noticed that he had found his own perfect spot. Lying flat on his back near the edge of the meadow, lazily maneuvering his kite above him, his face was a vision of happy contentment. Later he was able to admit with an open grin, "I had a *ball!"*

And so did we all. Weeks later, when any two of us met, we smiled and reminisced: *Wasn't that fun!*

* * *

The kite flight was far more gratifying then I ever envisioned. It was a perfect example of gifts given and received, and a charming metaphor for the holidays.

I wish for you two gifts this holiday season: *all* the simple pleasures, and *all* the camaraderie that this flying of kites symbolizes.

May the joy and blessings of Christmas be in your heart, wherever you happen to find yourself this year.

* * *

Oh, are you curious about a Second Annual Cushing Kite Flight? It's on for Labor Day weekend. Saturday, August 30, 2008, From 11 to 3. Rain and no-wind date, on the 31st.

Paper bag kite kits will be on hand, and Fales Store will serve hotdogs again. Kelly thinks we ought to have scoop ice cream too.

Will you join us?

We only have to wait for the mowing.

THE FRAGRANCE OF CHRISTMAS

People have celebrated the Winter Solstice for thousands of years. Ancient rituals seem to symbolize a battle between the forces of Light and Darkness. At long last, Darkness is overcome, and Light wins, as the sun again turns north -- a certain sign of hope and the expectation of coming spring.

What are the rituals of the season now? It's different for every family, of course. Over my own (lengthening!) lifetime, Christmas has always included my special people. We plan whose house to meet at, decide who is going to church, exchange gifts, sing carols, make phone calls to distant relatives, and delight in this year's marvelous tree, (decorated with baubles treasured through the years). We hang wreaths, light candles, read "The Littlest Angel," watch the movie, "It's a Wonderful Life," repeating a lot of the dialogue in unison! We prepare traditional foods. These things add to the rhythm of the holiday. The children always come first, because we think of Christmas as their day, while the older folk expect to relive poignant and joyful memories.

I remember especially my brother John and myself decorating our tree, just after the War ended. Probably it was 1945. John was 5; I was 10. My mother had bought new tinsel, a metal product that had been unavailable during the War Effort. We eagerly opened the flat little package, and simply stared. It wasn't shimmering strips of flexible silver, but hard, crimped strips that were difficult to bend. Draping pieces on the branches meant folding it double, but it was so stiff it remained a capital A. How we laughed to see this angular rain falling permanently sideways from our tree! We kept some to bring out again the following year, just for the humor of it.

Nowadays, on Christmas Eve, we all sit down to hear my daughter Caroline read "The Littlest Angel." I can't even attempt this myself, because I choke up by paragraph two. The children make appropriate remarks like, "C'mon, it's time to watch Gramma and Mom cry." I gleefully think to myself, "Just wait until you grow up, and have children of your own." I admire Caroline's fortitude. Sometimes she can delay her tears until page three.

The last thing the children do on Christmas Eve is to set out Christmas cookies and eggnog for Santa.
Large stockings, hung on the mantle, have waited patiently for several days for Santa to fill them. Coming safely (magically) down the chimney, he stuffs each of them with exquisite toys and other small things. Yes, a myriad rituals and traditions add to our comfort and pleasure.

* * *

Christmas Eve of 2007 was a bit subdued. Henry's brother Bryan and sister-in-law Christine were unable to join us as they usually do. We all missed them. It was after 8 o'clock when one of the children said, "It doesn't quite feel like Christmas."

Caroline asked, "What kind of things make it feel like Christmas?" That question started an animated discussion. Soon one of the children said, wistfully, "I miss the smell of poppy-seed cake."

Their mother apologized. "I decided against it, this year, since three of you have found out you're allergic to it."

The response was not at all what we expected. "We can bake it anyway," "Well, that's okay – I don't have to eat it." Andrew explained, "I know I can eat it if I want to, but I choose not to!"

Almost before we noticed, the children had disappeared into the kitchen. Food-preparation sounds commenced: the refrigerator door opening and closing, utensils clinking, the cracking of eggs, and the cheerful whir of the electric beater ringing against the side of the largest mixing bowl. Thank heaven a can of poppy-seed filling was in the pantry!

Caroline and Henry and I just grinned. I admit my mouth watered a little -- and yet I hadn't realized 'til that very moment that I'd been missing our poppy-seed cake!

* * *

So here it is. I was given this recipe when I was learning weaving techniques, 35 years ago, at Peter's Valley Craft Center, in New Jersey. This charming, historic village is filled with artists, and summer classes in many mediums such as blacksmithing, ceramics, weaving and jewelry. Check out: www.pvcrafts.org

PETER'S VALLEY POPPY-SEED CAKE

Pre-heat oven to 350°
4 eggs
3 cups flour
2 cups sugar
1 cup oil (like safflower)
1 teaspoon vanilla
½ teaspoon salt
1½ teaspoons baking soda
13 ounces evaporated milk

A 12 ounce can of poppy-seed filling
1 cup chopped nuts (optional)

First mix all ingredients together, except for the seeds and nuts.
Add seed filling. Beat at medium speed for 2 minutes.
Add chopped nuts

Pour into ungreased tube pan.
Bake for 70 minutes
Cool before removing from the pan.

Serve plain. Don't gild the lily!

* * *

The emotional tempo of the house shifted dramatically from subdued to super! Bustle and chatter and laughter increased. Even the dogs noticed, getting up from their naps to join the activity. Then Andrew settled on the piano bench and softly played Christmas carols with a light jazz touch, as the aroma of this traditional treat drifted throughout the house.

It took more than an hour to bake, and some time to allow it to cool. Then the cake was sliced for those who would eat it: Olivia, Caroline and me. It was marvelous indeed – dense and moist and rich and warm. "Oh my, yes, " I thought, "this is a Christmas tradition to keep!"

The abstainers -- Henry, Andrew and Sophie -- inhaled deeply of the fragrance. They seemed so pleased -- at least as satisfied as the partakers, and perhaps more so. These three had made us a truly special gift, knew its tasty value, and yet willingly denied themselves the pleasure. I am impressed by the spontaneous, nonchalant selflessness and generosity of these young people, my grandchildren. It is clear to me that the givers received the greater gift.

* * *

I wish you all the simple pleasures of this holiday.

May you experience, once again, the truth that it is more blessed to give than to receive.

* * *

$\mathcal{J}$UDITH M. $\mathcal{K}$NOWLTON

The author was born in Morristown, New Jersey in 1935. She is a graduate of Oberlin College, and was a Certified Addictions Counselor in New Jersey and Pennsylvania for 21 years.

Judy is the mother of three grown children and the grandmother of 6 grandchildren. Their names became several characters in this book: in memory of Jonathan, and to acknowledge Jenny and Maddie, and Andrew, Sophie and Olivia, who have climbed the Owl's Head Light stairs in the fog.

She has written several books on addictions and personal growth and is the owner of QUOTIDIAN PUBLISHERS - which means "One day at a time" in Latin.

A widow, and now retired, she and her two cats make their home in the town of Cushing, Maine.

A friend told her that she lives in the state where "People understand the correct use of long-handled spoons." She explains the reference this way: it is said that both heaven and hell are absolutely identical. In each, a magnificent banquet table is heaped with extra-ordinary delicacies and the most sumptuous food and drink. The people of heaven and hell gather around their tables with long-handled spoons strapped to their arms. In hell, the residents moan and wail into eternity because they are unable to feed and satisfy themselves.

But in heaven, the people graciously feed each other.

XXX

147

www.ingramcontent.com/pod-product-compliance
Lightning Source LLC
Chambersburg PA
CBHW070936130626
46555CB00001B/454